SAINT
SEBASTIAN'S
ABYSS

Also by Mark Haber

Reinhardt's Garden

SAINT
SEBASTIAN'S
ABYSS

Mark Haber

COFFEE HOUSE PRESS
Minneapolis
2022

The cover image is *Martyrdom of St. Sebastian* by Michael van Coxie.

Coffee House Press books are available to the trade through our primary distributor, Consortium Book Sales & Distribution, cbsd.com or (800) 283-3572. For personal orders, catalogs, or other information, write to info@coffeehousepress.org.

Coffee House Press is a nonprofit literary publishing house. Support from private foundations, corporate giving programs, government programs, and generous individuals helps make the publication of our books possible. We gratefully acknowledge their support in detail in the back of this book.

LIBRARY OF CONGRESS CATALOGING-IN-PUBLICATION DATA

Names: Haber, Mark, 1972– author.
Title: Saint Sebastian's abyss / Mark Haber.
Description: Minneapolis : Coffee House Press, [2022]
Identifiers: LCCN 2021056206 | ISBN 9781566896368 (paperback) |
    ISBN 9781566896443 (epub)
Subjects: LCGFT: Novels.
Classification: LCC PS3608.A23835 S25 2022 | DDC 813/.6—dc23
LC record available at https://lccn.loc.gov/2021056206

PRINTED IN THE UNITED STATES OF AMERICA
30 29 28 27 26 25 24 23   4 5 6 7 8 9 10 11

To Ülrika

"*Only a feeble light glimmers like a tiny star in a vast gulf of darkness. This feeble light is but a presentiment, and the soul, when it sees it, trembles in doubt whether the light is not a dream, and the gulf of darkness reality.*"

—Kandinsky, *Concerning the Spiritual in Art*

"*And I will give power unto my two witnesses.*"

—Revelation 11:3

SAINT
SEBASTIAN'S
ABYSS

1

After reading the email from Schmidt I knew I would have to fly to see Schmidt on his deathbed in Berlin. After rereading and reflecting on the more emphatic passages of his relatively short email, I was convinced I'd have to visit Schmidt one last time as he lay, in his words, dying in Berlin. Although we hadn't spoken in years, the email, sparse and cruel, hadn't surprised me; it felt suspended, as if it had been written years before and was merely waiting for me to open and read it. The tone of Schmidt's email hadn't surprised me either. Schmidt had been my best friend and confidant, my spiritual companion in art, art history, and art criticism, our interests drawn to the Northern Renaissance, specifically Dutch Mannerism and, more specifically than that, the painting *Saint Sebastian's Abyss* by Count Hugo Beckenbauer, *Saint Sebastian's Abyss* the focus of both our early studies and later our entire careers. Schmidt's guidance and affection and later our deep friendship were founded on our mutual love and adoration for *Saint Sebastian's Abyss*, at the time a little-known work by a little-known artist, hence all the more moving. We'd taken countless trips to Barcelona where *Saint Sebastian's Abyss* was (and still is) on display along with Beckenbauer's two lesser works. In Barcelona we beheld *Saint Sebastian's Abyss* in person, the first time to make sure the obsession we shared was authentic and every visit thereafter because of the obsession itself.

2

I read and reread Schmidt's relatively short email, going as far as printing it so I could underline specific passages during the long flight to Berlin. I printed three copies in fact; two for the flight and one to tuck in my luggage in the event of some mild misfortune: spilled coffee, a tear, pages forgotten in the restroom, and so on. I remembered I could always print a copy at the hotel in Berlin and for a moment felt silly, but this feeling passed because it would be absurd *not* to print something as vital as the deathbed missive from my spiritual and artistic confidant when I had the means at my disposal, thus I printed three copies to reread and underline, fold and unfold, disregard entirely if I felt like it, the choice was mine, the point being to *have a choice*, for I foresaw the next twelve hours as torment: soaring over the Atlantic condemned to the solitude of my own thoughts, no desire to read anything *but* the email, wholly occupied with studying, analyzing, construing (and likely misconstruing) all nine pages of Schmidt's relatively terse email, an email that, by the time we descended over Berlin, would no doubt be dog-eared and worn, pondered over and vigorously scrutinized because I hadn't spoken to my best friend, meaning Schmidt, in over ten years, thirteen to be exact, and Schmidt, being Schmidt, the less he said (or wrote), the more he revealed about art, art criticism, our once-brilliant devotion to each other, and our subsequent falling out, and, naturally, the most sublime painting in human history, *Saint Sebastian's Abyss.*

3

Schmidt had certain concrete ideas about art, the place of art in one's life, how art should be thought of and written about and even reflected upon in one's most private thoughts. Art, he believed, and I along with him, should be the centerpiece of one's entire world. Schmidt had no time for people who didn't hold art in the highest reverence and considered these people dim-witted and irrelevant, people, he felt, he had nothing in common with, no possible means of relating to, and hence even the shortest of conversations was a waste of time. Not revering art and not regarding art as the highest human accomplishment were immediate disqualifications for friendship. Of lesser concern were those who held art in the loftiest, most exalted position but were lazy or clumsy, incapable of writing, and thus thinking, about art. Schmidt pitied these people, for their hearts, he would say, were in the right place, as the expression went, but they lacked the intelligence to carry themselves with aplomb, and hence Schmidt pitied these types more than outright disqualifying them, though he didn't take them very seriously at all.

4

Schmidt famously hated both of my wives, my first and my second. He may have had a hand in the collapse of both of my marriages too. I say famously because Schmidt's hatred of both my first and my second wife was well-known among our circle of friends. When my first wife admitted to Schmidt over dinner that she didn't find art, painting in particular, especially compelling, Schmidt winced, set down his fork, and sighed dramatically; he then excused himself, explaining an appointment he'd forgotten about had suddenly and inexplicably been remembered, while making it abundantly clear there was no appointment at all.

5

Our decades-long friendship had crumbled when I'd said *that horrible thing.* What at the time I thought to be mild and innocuous, merely an opinion, was indeed, Schmidt was happy to tell me and later remind me, a *horrible thing,* a stain on my relatively scandal-free career, a major blunder and indiscretion that wouldn't be easily forgiven. I'd not only said *that horrible thing,* he said, but written it too, in my fourth book, *Serpent's Pastoral,* an exploration of the mythological imagery in *Saint Sebastian's Abyss,* and Schmidt took me to task for both writing and saying *that horrible thing,* later declaring, almost happily, that *that horrible thing* I'd said and then written would follow me for the rest of my career, which, in his opinion, had a rapidly approaching date of expiration. This didn't happen, and whatever Schmidt believed was horrible about *that horrible thing* I'd said and then written went largely unnoticed by academics, critics, artists, and even our friends. Moreover, the esteem in which my opinions were held only grew, and the more acclaim I received, the more Schmidt resented *that horrible thing* I'd said and then written regarding the most radiant painting in human history, *Saint Sebastian's Abyss,* something I couldn't take back, he'd insisted, since it was in writing too, in my fourth book, *Serpent's Pastoral,* and rehashed in my fifth book, *Harlequin's Affection.* I went on to write a sixth, seventh, and eighth book, all popular, and all dissecting different aspects of *Saint Sebastian's Abyss,* that glorious painting that had brought Schmidt and me together and likewise torn our friendship apart.

6

In our minds, there was nothing in the history of painting equal to *Saint Sebastian's Abyss* and every attempt at writing about it was merely a yearning for the ineffable, something transcendent that slunk away at each approach, both of us experiencing a sort of bleak satisfaction at the failure. This was all the more reason to write about *Saint Sebastian's Abyss*, we felt, because gazing at *Saint Sebastian's Abyss*, Schmidt was fond of saying, was like looking into the eyes of God, even though Schmidt and I didn't believe in God, Schmidt and I both fervent *nonbelievers*. I believe in art, Schmidt would say, I believe in oils and canvas and the *inherent finitude of human expression*. Schmidt also said that gazing at *Saint Sebastian's Abyss* was like having one's head lopped off with a long, dull blade. Look at the wings of the doves, he'd insist, look at the rays of apocalyptic light, he'd implore, and whether the apostles, the central motif of the painting, were indeed angels or prophets or messengers for good or ill, a subject of constant academic debate, was beside the point. Schmidt and I were obsessed with the apocalypse because we were obsessed with *Saint Sebastian's Abyss* and one couldn't be interested in *Saint Sebastian's Abyss* if one weren't also interested in the apocalypse since they were in conversation, a dance or a duel, no different than two mirrors facing one another, and sometimes Schmidt would press critics and historians who claimed to revere *Saint Sebastian's Abyss*, asking if they too loved the apocalypse or, at the very least, had a smattering of interest in the end of the world in all its radiant facades and this question, this *litmus test,* was the easiest way to determine whether a critic or art historian possessed any real reverence for *Saint Sebastian's Abyss* because relishing one (the painting) but not the other (the end of the world), Schmidt said, was unimaginable and akin, at least in his mind, to the highest philosophical transgression.

7

Sometimes Schmidt would stand in the shadows of the Rudolf Gallery in the Museu Nacional d'Art de Catalunya in Barcelona, afraid to get closer lest a *flood of emotions* overtake him. I fear the *flood of emotions* that will overtake me if I get near *Saint Sebastian's Abyss*, he'd say. If I step any closer to *Saint Sebastian's Abyss* I will lose myself, he'd declare, and I recall no fewer than three trips to Barcelona, to the Museu Nacional d'Art de Catalunya, more specifically to the Rudolf Gallery, where the guards and docents knew our faces and nodded respectfully without a word since they were well aware of our bodies of work, knew our obsession as well as the deference both Schmidt's and my writings on *Saint Sebastian's Abyss* afforded us, no fewer than three trips to visit, gaze at, and study *Saint Sebastian's Abyss* when Schmidt refused to visit, gaze at, study, or come anywhere near *Saint Sebastian's Abyss* for fear of his own emotions, what he termed a *flood of emotions*. It's not a religious painting, Schmidt maintained, and I agreed. But its *lack* of religion, he argued, is what makes the painting religious, almost super- or hyper-religious, and this *seeming religious* feeling, this so-called *pious* or *pious-adjacent* feeling, which overtook him no fewer than three times, was the reason, Schmidt claimed, he was forced to excuse himself. My first book, *Heaven's Purge*, delved into the religiosity of *Saint Sebastian's Abyss*, in other words, the *lack* of religion in *Saint Sebastian's Abyss*, because to believe, I'd written, one first had to surrender oneself to nonbelief, and *Saint Sebastian's Abyss*, with its sense of grief, its deep foreboding, its emissaries of doom, was the work of an artist in defiance of belief, therefore an artist in league with nonbelief.

8

Three trips to Barcelona, to the Museu Nacional d'Art de Catalunya, to the Rudolf Gallery where Schmidt would either stand adjacent to *Saint Sebastian's Abyss* or excuse himself entirely and on one of those three occasions I lost Schmidt, later to find Schmidt outside covered in perspiration, shoulders trembling, eyes vacant and aghast, blaming his absence on his *flood of emotions.* Later my first wife said Schmidt's *flood of emotions* was a performance, that Schmidt was feigning his *flood of emotions* to demonstrate that *Saint Sebastian's Abyss* touched and moved him more than it moved me, his *flood of emotions* nothing more than an act, she'd claimed, to prove he was more intimate with and devoted to and touched by *Saint Sebastian's Abyss* than I was. Later I too came to believe that Schmidt feigned his *flood of emotions* to demonstrate being touched more by *Saint Sebastian's Abyss* than I was, thus confirming, at least in his mind, that his understanding of *Saint Sebastian's Abyss* was deeper and more profound, to establish, at least in his mind, there were elements and details, emotions and subtleties in the work that escaped me. Sometimes, as we gazed at *Saint Sebastian's Abyss,* I would glance at Schmidt and see the eyes of a ghost.

9

Count Hugo Beckenbauer was born in Lower Saxony, along the Weser River, in 1512, the only child of impoverished pig farmers. He was never a count and added the title when he left Lower Saxony to pursue art. Becoming an artist was the last thing his parents expected of Hugo, who was not, in any way, a count, merely the child of, from what we can gather, miserable pig farmers. As far as we know Count Hugo Beckenbauer had no formal training as an artist, had no patrons or mentors to speak of. Count Hugo Beckenbauer left Lower Saxony at the age of seventeen, went first to Hameln, then to Brussels, then to Bremen, and finally to Berlin where he lived for the rest of his short life. Berlin is where I shall die, Schmidt would continually tell me, coughing, wheezing, dabbing his temples with a scarf, and now I was flying to Berlin to visit Schmidt on his deathbed.

10

Sometimes Schmidt would send me texts late at night, dark cryptic messages about the end of the world. Sometimes I would ignore these texts but just as often I would reply because Schmidt knew my weakness, knew I couldn't resist discussing the end of the world because Schmidt and I were insatiable when it came to talking about the end of the world. These text conversations could go on for hours, leading to telephone calls that inevitably became nightlong conversations about *Saint Sebastian's Abyss*—the first time we'd seen it in a book, the deep hues of burgundy, the nest of serpent's eggs, the omens brought to life by paint—and the next morning my second wife, who hated Schmidt as much as Schmidt hated my second wife, would see the color drained from my face, my eyes dry and devoid of sleep, and know I had been up all night talking to Schmidt about the end of the world, meaning we had been up all night talking about *Saint Sebastian's Abyss*. You've been talking to *that man* she would say, my second wife always referring to Schmidt as *that man*, making her in a sense more charitable than my first wife, who simply called Schmidt *asshole*, *jerkoff*, or *tedious prick*.

11

Schmidt hated anything new or modern, art especially. I was from the United States, a relatively new country, said Schmidt. Schmidt was from Austria, which he called an *ancient* country. Whenever Schmidt and I argued, invariably about art and more specifically about *Saint Sebastian's Abyss*, he would resort to calling the United States a second-rate nation and explain that, having been born and raised in the United States, unequivocally a second-rate nation, a lethargic infant of a society, a babbling baby of a drive-through culture, my opinions could only be infantile too, indulgent and crass and, like the United States, requiring centuries, perhaps epochs, to mature. My second wife was a professor of modern art and a critic of modern art. My second wife would gush about Lichtenstein and de Kooning and Frankenthaler just to watch Schmidt bristle and later categorically *curse* Lichtenstein and de Kooning and Frankenthaler. My second wife called Schmidt a luddite and Schmidt smiled, flexed his bushy mustache, and said if being a luddite meant having taste then he was, most certainly, a luddite. Schmidt told my second wife she had dedicated her life to *trash*. How does it feel, he'd ask her, to know you've dedicated your life to *trash*?

12

After I'd printed three copies of Schmidt's relatively short email I sat on the sofa to await my ride to the airport. I couldn't help but read the email once more, an email that appeared in my inbox like any other but bore the weight of a thousand lives. The tone and the words of the email, which were so Schmidt, drenched in *Schmidtisms*, accused me of countless misdeeds, of mediocrity and intellectual sluggishness, of not taking our friendship as seriously as he did; he called me a *typical moronic American* and once more brought up *that horrible thing* I'd said, now so long ago, first out loud and then in my fourth book, *Serpent's Pastoral*, and then, a little later, in my fifth book, *Harlequin's Affection*, that *horrible thing*, which, he'd claimed, was both senseless and absurd. Schmidt also gloated about how he would die in Berlin, as he had predicted, just as Max Liebermann and Adolph Menzel and Carl Blechen and countless other artists had died in Berlin, but most important among them, Count Hugo Beckenbauer. Berlin is the resting place of the greatest minds, he wrote, meaning, principally, Count Hugo Beckenbauer and himself.

13

Count Hugo Beckenbauer was what we today would call *flamboyant*. He enjoyed wearing a long velvet cape, riding boots, and a plumed hat while prancing around Berlin in the early 1500s. By 1532 he had lived in Berlin for three years. He had likely contracted syphilis soon after arriving, a disease that would later ravage his mind, although he had several years of productive work ahead of him, a period that yielded prints, sketches, and an abundant body of paintings of which the greatest, *Saint Sebastian's Abyss*, thankfully survived. A rough contemporary of Pieter Bruegel the Elder, Beckenbauer preceded the Early Renaissance yet was in conversation with the Early Renaissance, influencing it in ways that Schmidt and I were the first to discover. Though a known teetotaler, Count Hugo Beckenbauer adored Berlin for its atmosphere congenial to intellectual and artistic pursuits and whenever he sold a painting he spent his money at the brothels and bordellos of Berlin's murkier districts, purchasing sex from both women and young boys since Count Hugo Beckenbauer, though strictly not a drinker, was indiscriminate when it came to sexual partners. Count Hugo Beckenbauer was probably what we today would call a *sex addict*.

14

Saint Sebastian's Abyss is twelve inches by fourteen, a small painting no doubt, Beckenbauer's smallest surviving work in fact. It was painted in a barn outside Düsseldorf during one of Beckenbauer's rare spells of lucidity. Düsseldorf was the city Beckenbauer escaped to when running from various debts and debt collectors. Once he'd completed a few paintings he returned to Berlin to sell his work, satisfy his debts, and fornicate. By his late twenties the syphilis had taken much of the use of his left hand and severely marred his outward appearance; several extant narratives describe a wearied Beckenbauer tramping the dusty streets in search of a lover, his milky eyes peering from beneath a horsehair blanket, a walking stick tapping the dry earth in front of him. Beckenbauer became notorious in both Düsseldorf and Berlin, in the brothels especially, where Beckenbauer wasn't above offering panels, portraiture, and meager wooden sculptures in exchange for the slightest acts of intimacy and one can only speculate if Beckenbauer painted in order to have sex or had sex to galvanize himself for the works emblazoned upon his mind's eye, cacophonous sketches of yawning ravines and ecstatic martyrs, the sacred ruins of a once-glorious paradise, works that disturbed as well as delighted and of which the greatest, *Saint Sebastian's Abyss*, thankfully endured.

15

In the lower left field of *Saint Sebastian's Abyss*, where the cliff's edge meets the foot of the holy donkey, the initials WFG sit awkwardly. Schmidt and I spent decades trying to discover the origins of this mysterious dedication with no success, countless hours greedily scouring historical documents in archives across Europe and finding no trace, no hint of what the three letters signified. Beckenbauer's signature, with its rising arch and grandiloquent flourish, sits on the bottom right corner, just as it does in his other surviving paintings, the two lesser works Schmidt and I avoided talking about, and the various papers he signed during his short life, which Schmidt and I found in both the Düsseldorf and Berlin tax offices along with subpoenas, court records, and public complaints regarding his various moral transgressions. These initials bewitched as much as frustrated us, three letters with no apparent meaning, containing implications both baffling and obscure, letters that Schmidt pledged to discover even if it was the last thing he were to do. Even if it's the last thing I do, Schmidt once confided, circling the benches in the Parc de la Fontsanta, exercising his sick lungs, flapping his arms like a maimed bird, I will discover the context and significance of the initials WFG.

16

Schmidt's favorite painting after *Saint Sebastian's Abyss* was *Minerva Victorious over Ignorance* by Bartholomeus Spranger, not because of its subject or theme, he would say, but its use of light, or, in Schmidt's words, *the dramatic use of color that cultivates mystery*. Schmidt and I were obsessed with the use of light. We were also obsessed with the use of dark. We were obsessed with shadows. We were obsessed with open space and, at the same time, teeming space. We were obsessed with ambiguity, irony, and the intricacy of devotion, though not a religious devotion but a devotion to art, especially art that detailed the apocalypse. We were obsessed with paint, oils, pigments, canvas, and the viscera of painting. We were especially obsessed with Early Netherlandish painting and Dutch Mannerism and if we hadn't stumbled upon Count Hugo Beckenbauer in the back of a little-known textbook assigned to us at Oxford, at the Ruskin School, where Schmidt and I met, our lives would have certainly followed different paths, most likely the paths of studying either Early Netherlandish painting or Dutch Mannerism because next to Count Hugo Beckenbauer and *Saint Sebastian's Abyss* there was nothing Schmidt and I loved more than Early Netherlandish painting and Dutch Mannerism. But we *did* stumble upon *Saint Sebastian's Abyss* in the back of our textbook at Oxford, at the Ruskin School, where we met, a miracle, a masterwork, a trembling jewel that, were it not for me and Schmidt, our discovery would've remained a mere footnote in the world of Renaissance Art, hence stumbling upon *Saint Sebastian's Abyss* changed not only the course of our lives but forever transformed the world of Renaissance Art criticism.

17

My favorite painting after *Saint Sebastian's Abyss* is *The Conversion of Saint Paul* by Caravaggio. Schmidt enjoyed ridiculing my second favorite painting, comparing his second favorite painting, *Minerva Victorious over Ignorance,* to my second favorite painting, explaining why his second favorite painting was superior to my second favorite painting. Schmidt called Caravaggio melodramatic. Schmidt accused me of fetishizing and dimensionalizing Caravaggio. Schmidt said he well understood why Caravaggio would appeal to someone like me, an incurious American toddler nursed on the teats of an illiterate culture. He sympathized with my need for signposts and symbolism, because, being an American, he'd said, I couldn't help myself, being an American, he hastened to add, I'd been stunted and impaired and because of this *geographical shortcoming* I suffered a lack of nutrients readily found in the *ancient soils of Europe,* Austria especially, its soil as dark and rich and awash with history as one could ever dream of, the complete inverse of the *anemic American soil* on which I'd regrettably been raised, he'd said, a *wasteland,* he'd called it, a *revolting abyss,* he'd added, a nation whose ground was utterly devoid of nutritional benefits, bereft of any sustenance at all, a dirt no doubt replete with candy wrappers and condoms and the residue of all manner of crimes, but not art, not history, not the fundamental ingredients required for the temperament of an important critic.

18

The Great Stockholm Fire of 1625 lasted three days and destroyed all Count Hugo Beckenbauer's paintings besides *Saint Sebastian's Abyss* and the two lesser works that we tried not to talk about. His entire oeuvre had been purchased by a Swedish collector whose home burned in the blaze, killing the collector's wife and three sons. Everything Beckenbauer had painted in Berlin and at the Düsseldorf farmhouse amidst his late-stage syphilis was incinerated besides *Saint Sebastian's Abyss* and the two lesser paintings that survived, miraculously intact. Sometimes Schmidt and I imagined what the rest of Beckenbauer's paintings had looked like. I imagined works of profound allegory, paintings that invoked spiritual transformation through formal ecstasy. Schmidt imagined a collection of dull and uninspired landscapes, bales of hay or limpid streams or perhaps hungry peasants, all painted by a sufferer of late-stage syphilis sliding into a schism of madness and grief. There could be no greater work by Count Hugo Beckenbauer than *Saint Sebastian's Abyss*, Schmidt insisted, and I agreed because agreeing with Schmidt was easier than disagreeing with Schmidt. Still, I envisioned works *greater* than *Saint Sebastian's Abyss* because while I sought and entertained the possible, Schmidt eschewed and cursed the possible, meaning he courted and invited the impossible.

19

Schmidt and I avoided thinking and talking and writing about Count Hugo Beckenbauer's two lesser works for as long as possible until, after a series of successful books and lectures, it became impossible for us *not* to think, talk, and eventually write about Count Hugo Beckenbauer's two lesser works. Both of us agreed Beckenbauer's two lesser works were quite mediocre, in fact Schmidt considered them abominable. In private Schmidt referred to Beckenbauer's two lesser works as his *monkey paintings*, implying that a monkey could have painted them. In public, however, we were more forgiving. Schmidt and I enjoyed much success thinking and talking and writing about Beckenbauer and *Saint Sebastian's Abyss*, both of us credited with discovering a little-known master and we knew we would one day have to discuss his two lesser works, the *monkey paintings* as Schmidt privately called them. Eventually we did think and talk and write about Beckenbauer's two lesser works in very generous terms, taking into consideration the period of time, the late-stage syphilis, the debts Beckenbauer was running from, and other details, always approaching them with a certain benevolence, endeavoring, meanwhile, to discuss *Saint Sebastian's Abyss* as much as possible, often making it the focus, thus showing the two lesser works (or the *monkey paintings*) in a better light. In Paris, at the Centre Pompidou, we spoke of *Saint Sebastian's Abyss* for a total of two hours and the two lesser works, collectively, for less than fifteen minutes because discussing or even thinking about the two lesser works, or the *monkey paintings*, Schmidt confided, demeaned and cheapened and besmirched the only work that mattered, meaning *Saint Sebastian's Abyss*, and there's a very good chance, he'd conclude, that talking about the two lesser works, in essence neglecting talking about *Saint Sebastian's Abyss*, was *destroying his soul* and then Schmidt, his mustache drenched, his lungs emitting a low, damp whistle, would embark on his daily constitutional.

20

The two lesser paintings that survived the Great Stockholm Fire were untitled. At first Schmidt and I referred to these works as the *two lesser works that we try not to talk about* simply because we did not, in any way, relish talking about them. Later we began calling the two untitled paintings the *monkey paintings* after Schmidt declared that a monkey could have painted them and he and I shared a laugh as we often did in the early years before Schmidt contributed to the ruin of both of my marriages and before I'd said and later written *that horrible thing.* I often wish only *Saint Sebastian's Abyss* had survived the fire, Schmidt would say and I'd agree. The *two lesser works that we try not to talk about,* which later became, at least to Schmidt and me, the *monkey paintings,* were indeed bad paintings, objectively bad, works that attempted to annihilate the glory and prestige of *Saint Sebastian's Abyss* merely by existing. Moreover, the *two lesser works that we tried not to talk about,* or the *monkey paintings,* made the attention bestowed upon Beckenbauer's masterwork difficult to justify. If the man was as brilliant as Schmidt and I made our careers claiming, we'd tell ourselves (playing the devil's advocate), how could he have painted *these*? Still, people who knew very little or even less lauded and appreciated the two lesser works. A person or group of persons had in fact determined that the two lesser works were good enough to hang in the Rudolf Gallery in the Museu Nacional d'Art de Catalunya in Barcelona, looming on both sides of *Saint Sebastian's Abyss* no less, though Schmidt admitted in private that if it were up to him he would've happily burned them, burned them with glee and without thinking twice and kept the ashes too, he'd said, in an urn that he'd place prominently on a mantel in the Berlin residence he hoped one day to die in, an urn that would serve as a reminder of the perils and pitfalls of mediocrity.

21

In contrast to *Saint Sebastian's Abyss*, the *two lesser works that we tried not to talk about*, or the *monkey paintings*, are enormous, looming large and abhorrent on both sides of *Saint Sebastian's Abyss* like unreasonable siblings, bullying and bookending their brilliant baby brother. I think the *monkey paintings* exist to remind us of the depravity of the world, Schmidt once said. I think the *monkey paintings* exist, I replied, to remind us of death. The *monkey paintings* surely exist to counterbalance the transcendence and sublimity of *Saint Sebastian's Abyss*, Schmidt said in turn, to illustrate the mediocrity of this world, how mediocrity looms larger and, in essence, ruins things because mediocrity always inevitably ruins things, and Schmidt would continue in this vein for quite a while because nothing excited Schmidt more than talking about mediocrity and how it inevitably ruins things. Mediocrity is a disease that will always win, he'd say, has always won, and will continue to win or, at the very least, have the upper hand, mediocrity, he'd said, which is terrible at excellence and sublimity and true beauty, since they are its opposites of course, but *absolutely peerless* at outsmarting and hence repressing the exceptional, thus mediocrity is superlative at spreading and proliferating and, because of this, because of mediocrity's unrivaled capacity for annihilating beauty, it will always be victorious. Schmidt and I both resented Count Hugo Beckenbauer's two untitled paintings, the *monkey paintings*, the two lesser works that we tried not to talk about for as long as possible until the critics and scholars, in fact the entire world of art, could stand it no longer and demanded we think, talk, and write about Count Hugo Beckenbauer's two lesser works, works that, to Schmidt and me, lacked any formal seriousness and were merely distractions, antagonists and enemies of beauty.

22

Saint Sebastian's Abyss, like all masterworks, contains multitudes. It's *drenched* in color but entirely *devoid* of color. It's not a landscape though it's certainly pastoral. It's not religious though it's bursting with religious symbolism: apostles, iconography, the holy donkey, a sky rent by divine lightning. To try and describe *Saint Sebastian's Abyss* in words is an act of futility, thus the allure *Saint Sebastian's Abyss* held for a young Schmidt and me when we came across a small reproduction of *Saint Sebastian's Abyss* buried in our textbook at Oxford, at the Ruskin. Perched on adjoining desks, Schmidt and I had been chatting about the end of the world while flipping through our textbook, a tedious tome that devoted far too much attention to Titian and the Hermitage. I came across the reproduction of *Saint Sebastian's Abyss* crouched at the bottom of the page and paused, though Schmidt likes to claim *he* came across the reproduction first and paused. I saw the image first, he always asserted, I nudged you just as you turned the page. I, however, remember the moment exactly as Schmidt described it but the other way around. I turned and I saw and I nudged, not Schmidt. Still, we were moved by the reproduction and asked our professor about Count Hugo Beckenbauer and more specifically about *Saint Sebastian's Abyss* and the professor either didn't know anything or had no interest because he merely shrugged and instructed us to continue working on our papers, mine devoted to Early Netherlandish panels and Schmidt's concentrating on Rembrandt and the Symbolism of Crisis.

23

The car arrived to take me to the airport, to the plane that would eventually land in Berlin where Schmidt lay on his deathbed. I folded the two copies of Schmidt's terse email and put them in my jacket pocket as the city went by in a blur of neon and noise. My second wife often laughed at *that horrible thing* I'd said, telling me it wasn't horrible at all, that it was merely an opinion and an honest opinion at that. Schmidt's evident rage at *that horrible thing* I had both said and written was preposterous, she'd said, as it was merely me choosing a side, something a person was forced to do in the world of art, to state an opinion, postulate a theory, and then stand behind it with all the fortitude and tenacity one could gather. Schmidt wants you to fail, she would say, your failure would be the biggest success of his life. Not long after I'd said and written *that horrible thing* Schmidt began behaving differently. The beginning of the end, I later realized, was *that horrible thing*. My second wife thought very little of our disagreement, considered it temporary, called it a *spat*. She wouldn't understand, I'd told myself, obsessed as she was with modernism, abstract art, and feminist theory. Her views held no history, I'd thought, they contained no sense of painting's scope, whereas Schmidt's heart and my own heart carried the breadth of centuries. Had she, I'd reasoned, ever considered the end of the world? Had my second wife, I'd mused, ever studied the violence in *Saint Sebastian's Abyss*, felt the weight of humanity's sins upon her shoulders?

Had my second wife ever stared into the eyes of the holy donkey standing on the precipice, head cast toward the viewer, its feeble hooves unstable on blackened pebbles, and seen reflected back her own abstract horror?

24

Schmidt and I often visited museums where Schmidt would click his tongue violently at the modern art. Schmidt didn't approve of modern art but enjoyed clicking his tongue violently at modern art. Schmidt would famously say that painting almost died in 1528 with the death of Matthias Grünewald but was saved by Early Netherlandish painting, Dutch Mannerism, and the Renaissance. Art most assuredly died once and for all, he'd say, in 1906 with the death of Cézanne. In 1906 painting died once and for all, he'd proclaim, it nearly died in 1528 but was resuscitated, heaving and disfigured, to be salvaged and reclaimed by Early Netherlandish painting, Dutch Mannerism, and the Renaissance. It survived, indeed, *thrived,* he'd explain to me as well as anyone in proximity, through the baroque and further, until Cézanne's death in 1906. Everything that came after was either not art or worse, *trash.* Still, he'd say, we can at least amuse ourselves with this *trash.* It's an empirical fact, he once declared, that any artist who was alive on December 31, 1905, stopped being an artist at midnight, that is, they awoke on January 1, 1906—a Monday I believe—and were no longer artists, hence everything they painted thereafter was not art and most likely *trash.* Schmidt said cubism gave him hives. Schmidt claimed abstract expressionism was a mental disorder. Schmidt said Cubo-futurism and Dadaism were the work of monsters. He behaved very differently at museums that didn't house *Saint Sebastian's Abyss,* meaning every museum in the world besides the Museu Nacional d'Art de Catalunya in Barcelona.

25

The first of the two untitled paintings, meaning the first of the two *monkey paintings*, stands eight feet by twenty in the Rudolf Gallery in the Museu Nacional d'Art de Catalunya in Barcelona. Suspended to the left of *Saint Sebastian's Abyss* like an eager hunchback with an overbite, it is soaked in bruised reds and amethyst, depicting, it appears, a tumbrel in the foreground of a wooded path. The tumbrel, delineated in dense brushstrokes of coarse brown, evokes both pain and urgency, mostly for the viewer. Of constant speculation is what the tumbrel (or wheelbarrow) is carrying. At first glance it appears to be heads of corn but on closer inspection Schmidt and I were convinced it was sacks of seed or a grain of some sort and Schmidt's third book, *The Descent*, spent several chapters illustrating why the tumbrel, or wheelbarrow, contained sacks of seed and not corn. The painting weaves touches of naturalism into the grotesque and the viewers can't be sure if the feeling of repulsion that overcomes them—or at least overcame Schmidt and me—was intentional or happenstance. There's little craft in the representation of the tumbrel and the wooded path, which both come across as flat and undeveloped, rather an exhibition of incompetence, for one sees in the tumbrel and the wooded path not nature or a reflection of reality but an anemic artist reaching for something he'll never grasp. The flaccid strokes, the ill-chosen colors, all suggest a feeble talent. Adding to the horror is the frame itself: golden, cloying, a testament to bad taste or a lack of good taste, which amounts to the same thing. Sometimes when we visited *Saint Sebastian's Abyss* we were forced to cup our hands on both sides of our faces to block out both the first and the second *monkey paintings* and to hem in the most sublime act of human glory, *Saint Sebastian's Abyss*. Some art historians asserted that both the first and the second untitled works were painted around the same time as *Saint Sebastian's Abyss*, which was something Schmidt and I could not abide since the notion that those atrocities could have been created in the same year, the same decade even, nauseated our very souls. Truth be told, the idea that they were painted by the same *man* was something Schmidt and I would forever wrestle with and rare was the time we didn't consider the two lesser works without disgust scratching the backs of our throats.

26

According to some critics Count Hugo Beckenbauer's two lesser works implied that the grandeur and sublimity of *Saint Sebastian's Abyss* were *unintended*, an aberration, a flame of visionary light, and this was something Schmidt could not live with. I cannot endure the idea that *Saint Sebastian's Abyss* was an act of chance, Schmidt would say, it's something I can't reconcile, for imagine creating something as sublime as *Saint Sebastian's Abyss* by *accident!* Schmidt and I were both plagued by the perfection of *Saint Sebastian's Abyss* just as we were plagued by the mediocrity of his two lesser works, his *monkey paintings*, which surrounded *Saint Sebastian's Abyss* and harried *Saint Sebastian's Abyss* and persecuted the small frame of *Saint Sebastian's Abyss* simply by their ludicrous placement, so close to the greatest painting of all time, panting heavily on both sides of *Saint Sebastian's Abyss* like idiot bystanders or thwarted rapists who, seeing the beauty beside them, perceive their own hideous hearts. *Saint Sebastian's Abyss* should have its own wall, we agreed, perhaps its own gallery, we also agreed, even its own museum, we agreed thirdly, though we knew that was taking it too far. Still, to share the same wall as those two monstrosities, we thought, was not just insulting, it was sacrilege. Let's call the two lesser works what they truly are, Schmidt exhorted in private, *abominations*. The unassailable beauty of *Saint Sebastian's Abyss* was so at odds with the two lesser works that for years Schmidt entertained outlandish schemes of extraction, even breaking into the museum, into the Rudolf Gallery, and destroying both works though Schmidt, never possessing the strongest constitution, knew this was impossible for when Schmidt wasn't writing about *Saint Sebastian's Abyss* or ruminating on *Saint Sebastian's Abyss* or speaking about *Saint Sebastian's Abyss* he was recovering from an attack of asthma or his litany of autoimmune diseases including Guillain-Barré syndrome and, when afflicted, Schmidt would take various rest cures in spa towns he had haunted since his youth, resorts and thermal baths skirting the Black Forest and sprinkled across Austria and, decades later, private hospitals in Berlin where I was now flying to see him on his deathbed.

27

At Oxford, at the Ruskin School, Schmidt and I became fast friends due to our mutual fascination with the end of the world and, soon after, our discovery of *Saint Sebastian's Abyss*, a painting that, in our opinion, *illustrated* the end of the world, because one couldn't gaze at the hems of the apostles or look into the eyes of the holy donkey or, likewise, ponder the dark smudges of bruised sky and not consider the apocalypse or Armageddon, in short, the end-times, because Schmidt and I were quenchless and insatiable when it came to the end of the world. Our classmates were only interested in becoming painters, which was preposterous since nothing good had been painted since the death of Cézanne in 1906. Painting, I told Schmidt, admittedly to impress him, was a fool's errand because painting had died with Cézanne in 1906 and to pursue painting was like pursuing an obsolete skill, becoming a chimney sweep or a town crier, completely at odds with the contemporary world and though Schmidt and I may have come across as antiquated, we were citizens of the contemporary world, we lived and breathed in the contemporary world, enough to realize painting was dead and what was left, of course, was *writing* about painting and we chose to dedicate our lives to *writing* about painting, specifically *Saint Sebastian's Abyss*. With every trip to the Museu Nacional d'Art de Catalunya in Barcelona, we felt more like archaeologists visiting an excavation site, every glimpse of *Saint Sebastian's*

Abyss akin to opening a glorious sarcophagus for when we looked upon the pensive skies liked bruised fruit and the nest of serpent's eggs and the vines along the escarpment, our souls wept, souls pleading to be released from the mediocrity of the world and sometimes, if Schmidt wasn't around, if Schmidt had gone outside to cough or exercise his lungs by traipsing in circles, I'd literally weep at the foot of the painting, certain I'd always understood *Saint Sebastian's Abyss* on a deeper and more devotional level than Schmidt.

28

I'm not always certain what art is, Schmidt was fond of saying, but I'm always certain what art *isn't*. This was said at exhibits around the world where Schmidt and I had been invited to speak. Walking by the paintings, clicking his tongue violently, Schmidt informed anyone in earshot that what they were looking at was invariably not art, and there was a good chance, he added, that it was *trash*. The difference between something being not art and being *trash* was practically indiscernible and sometimes Schmidt deemed a painting not art only to turn around and correct himself by calling it *trash*. Other times, albeit rarely, Schmidt would call a work *trash* only to later backtrack by saying it was simply not art. Art is rare, we agreed, because humanity no longer produces artists; we live in a world of monotonous excrement or excremental monotony, we'd say, the difference being immaterial because the point being the world is awash with monotony while simultaneously overflowing with excrement, excrement and monotony bursting from every direction, a world that has not dulled or impaired but, in fact, *annihilated* the inspiration necessary to create artists, anything even remotely resembling the inspiration necessary to create artists has been wholly annihilated. Artists are akin to those giant tortoises from the Galápagos Islands, we'd conclude, those enormous turtles that have gone extinct and will never return.

29

Sometimes while giving exclusive tours at the Rudolf Gallery I was caught cupping my hands on both sides of my face to block out the *monkey paintings*. I explained this as a common practice among the best art historians. Indeed, I'd tell my listeners, Schmidt does the very same thing as it provides the focus and absorption the great masters deserve. My listeners would follow suit, cupping their hands to both sides of their faces, but applying this maneuver to the *monkey paintings*, an act of useless absurdity, essentially blocking out the most majestic and elevated painting in human history instead of applying it to the only painting that demanded the blocking out of bad art, mediocrity, and thus, the rest of the world, *Saint Sebastian's Abyss*.

30

Schmidt and I enjoyed success at a very early age. Barely out of Oxford, hardly out of the Ruskin School, we were quickly lauded, given equal credit for having discovered (or rediscovered) Count Hugo Beckenbauer and *Saint Sebastian's Abyss*. Our books on Beckenbauer and *Saint Sebastian's Abyss* were called *revelatory* and *groundbreaking* and not only compelling but *utterly compelling*, our books having, in one critic's words, *redefined art theory and art criticism regarding the Early Renaissance*. We were amazed at the amount of money museums and institutes and universities would pay to hear us speak since Schmidt and I were still relatively young. At the time we were the only authorities on Count Hugo Beckenbauer and *Saint Sebastian's Abyss*, though much later several critics followed in our path. Their work, however, was anemic and bloodless, lacking the passion, some might say the obsession, that Schmidt and I had in spades. Two books put out by each of us in as many years grappling with the *cosmic ecstasy* of *Saint Sebastian's Abyss* as well as the *oppression* of *Saint Sebastian's Abyss*, for the painting, we wrote, invigorated as much as it destroyed, inspired as much as it tormented, it was a work as innocent as it was guilty, as meaningful as it was meaningless. Much like life, Schmidt was fond of saying, *Saint Sebastian's Abyss* is utterly mercurial and reaches out even as it slaps your hand, meaning the viewer's hand, away. I stand before *Saint Sebastian's Abyss*, I'd often say, and *Saint Sebastian's*

Abyss is a different painting each time. This spoken before crowds at the Louvre and the Smithsonian and the Tate; we flew to Amsterdam and Lisbon and Buenos Aires where Schmidt, ambling beside the works in the Museo Fortabat, clicked his tongue violently at the contemporary art, steadfast and unafraid, stridently name-calling and criticizing, labeling all of it *rubbish* and *eyesores* and *trash,* insinuating these *artists,* and here he spewed the word *artists* with all the vitriol at his formidable command, reveling as always in his own grandiloquence, these *artists,* he spewed, lack scholarship and discipline, these so-called *artists,* he raved, are better suited to painting houses or fences, perhaps working for the local government on the side of the highway in a beautification project, yes, that's it, an overpass, these *artists* should be painting or decorating an overpass! Schmidt's first book, *August in Rhapsody,* dealt with the mystical ecstasy of *Saint Sebastian's Abyss* and was followed fourteen months later by *The Gospels of Count Hugo* and despite these titles, Schmidt's books and my books were not about religion but about the godlessness and impiety and *lack* of religion in *Saint Sebastian's Abyss* because Schmidt and I were not only staunch adherents to secular art criticism but brazen and devout nonbelievers and instead of God we believed in art, preferably art that illustrated the end of the world.

31

Almost everything we know about Count Hugo Beckenbauer's life in Düsseldorf is taken from the journals of his landlady, Helga Heidel, who, by our good fortune, kept a comprehensive diary. Helga Heidel was a widow, childless, a benevolent soul who nursed Beckenbauer during the fevers and visions he suffered during his late-stage syphilis while keeping a detailed account of her daily life, three full journals that illustrate Beckenbauer's habits as a painter, his *episodes*, as Heidel calls them, and eventually his exclusion from the town. According to Heidel, Beckenbauer was known to walk the muddy streets of Düsseldorf once the summer storms had passed, talking to spirits or demons and courting mystical visions. Beckenbauer often grew agitated during these otherworldly encounters and landowners and village officers would be forced to intervene, sometimes finding Beckenbauer in the woods wearing only his plumed hat and riding boots. It wasn't long before Beckenbauer became a pariah. On one particular visit, writes Heidel, Beckenbauer returned from Berlin with a prostitute whom, he insisted, he planned to marry. This didn't stop him from ogling the local women and chasing young boys and, if the venereal fevers were strong enough, defecating in the street. The prostitute left after a few days, Heidel writes, not angry or upset, but simply bored with the countryside. Her return to Berlin, writes Heidel, left Hugo bereft. She writes: *The poor man has known the harlot only a week's time and still he suffers. He throws himself into his worst vices, giving himself over to every base instinct, chasing women and hanging around the schoolyard. A sort of irrational frenzy overtakes him and when he deems himself ready to paint, they're small and brutal works, beastly caricatures of the locals with the addition of horns or tails and when I inquire about what he's painted he mutters that he paints exactly what he sees, which, he maintains, is the divine messenger of the apocalypse.* Heidel adds that this *madness* often preceded the genuinely creative periods when he would take residence in her farmhouse to paint enormous canvases using chalk, egg yolk, and various homemade oils. Our knowledge of the details and indeed the existence of Beckenbauer's other works derives solely from Heidel's diaries. Sadly, the Swedish art collector who later purchased Beckenbauer's entire body of work kept no records, or if he did, they burned with the rest of his family in 1625 and as a consequence there exists no provenance for *Saint Sebastian's Abyss.* Likewise the first and only catalogue raisonné of Count Hugo Beckenbauer was authored by Schmidt and me shortly after our departure from Oxford and the Ruskin School, our catalogue raisonné in fact the only publication we coauthored, our debut upon the world stage, before the productive years, before the countless successes and controversies and the ugly collapse of both of my marriages and finally, perhaps inevitably, our subsequent falling out.

32

Schmidt's first book, *August in Rhapsody*, was highly celebrated in the world of art criticism, which was happy to laud and acclaim a new voice (always in the hope of one day celebrating the downfall of that new voice). *August in Rhapsody* contained a preface by me just as my first three books contained a preface by Schmidt. We often prefaced or wrote afterwords and addendums to one another's work to demonstrate, especially to the world of art, that two separate minds could agree on the greatest painting in history while approaching the work in distinctive ways. I, for example, believed *Saint Sebastian's Abyss* was the greatest painting in history because of its use of color, light, and the suggestion of a benevolent apocalypse. Schmidt, conversely, felt that *Saint Sebastian's Abyss* was the greatest painting in history because of its mastery of perspective as well as technique. Schmidt was obsessed with technique and *August in Rhapsody* was a book wholly fixated on the technique involved in *Saint Sebastian's Abyss;* Schmidt put forth some very contentious and groundbreaking arguments in justifying the technique used in *Saint Sebastian's Abyss,* painted in the Düsseldorf farmhouse, Beckenbauer suffering from late-stage syphilis, partially or completely blind, sex-obsessed and with only a functioning right hand, all explained in comprehensive, almost exhaustive detail with nothing left out, no stone unturned, no argument untested because Schmidt believed every approach *should* be tested and every stone turned, and thus Schmidt's first book, *August in Rhapsody*, was over twelve hundred pages including rambling meditations on technique, philosophical digressions on death, and a detailed account of why *Saint Sebastian's Abyss* was the greatest painting in human history.

33

My first wife demanded we see a marriage counselor. My first wife claimed my love and adoration for Schmidt and, by extension, *Saint Sebastian's Abyss*, was exasperating and when she was talking, she maintained, I wasn't there, my eyes drifting and taking on a hazy film, and when she spoke she knew I wasn't listening but rather reflecting on Schmidt or *Saint Sebastian's Abyss* or the end of the world or perhaps all three because, she asserted, I had a defect, a human glitch, that made me think only of Schmidt or *Saint Sebastian's Abyss* or the end of the world or perhaps all three. You care more about that fucking painting than you do about me, she'd said, and I made no response or if I did I can no longer recall what it was. I refused to see a marriage counselor though, and not long afterward I left on a lecture tour for my second book, *Hem of the Apostles*, a book that examined the use of opaque light and flickering shadow in the hems of the apostles in *Saint Sebastian's Abyss*, the centerpiece or nucleus of the work, a subject of endless fascination and surely my second favorite aspect of the painting after the holy donkey and when I returned from my lecture tour my first wife had not only left the country but sued me for divorce.

34

Schmidt made a lot of enemies by calling art not art or *trash*. Many of these artists were still alive and took obvious offense at Schmidt's ridiculing or dismissing their work as not art or *trash* and would, in turn, ridicule or dismiss *Saint Sebastian's Abyss* thus invalidating Schmidt's entire life's work. I tried avoiding these fueds but at various lectures and symposiums was asked my opinion of Schmidt's comments and if I agreed that all art, especially after 1906, was *trash*? Looking back, it seems inevitable, peppered as I was by constant questions, that I would one day say *that horrible thing* and finally I did, in answer to a question at a conference, and shortly thereafter I included *that horrible thing* in my next book, *Serpent's Pastoral* and, a little later, reiterated *that horrible thing* in another book, *Harlequin's Affection*, having no idea Schmidt would find it such *a horrible thing*, horrible enough that he would divorce himself from our friendship, dissolve and relinquish our entire history, not making it immediately apparent but doing it in stages, over three or four years, making subtle comments at first to me or my second wife, so only much later, looking back, did I realize *that horrible thing* was what offended him, offended him so much that Schmidt was compelled to reexamine our entire history, exhaustively so, two decades long at that point, although he sometimes implied that perhaps that thing I'd said and later written could be taken back, redressed and apologized for, though he never brought it up directly. And when I did finally realize that *that horrible thing* I'd both said and written was the cause of our rupture it was too late; I had said and written too many things supporting *that horrible thing* to ever go back.

35

The first time Schmidt and I beheld *Saint Sebastian's Abyss* in person we were overwhelmed. Still students, we had borrowed the money to fly from England to Spain with no plan for how to pay it back. In the Rudolf Gallery we stood before the work, stock-still, our nerves thrumming, our souls vanquished, conquered by what Schmidt called *the inexhaustible superabundance* of *Saint Sebatsian's Abyss*—the color and craft, the quiet violence, the hallucinatory brushstrokes that felt, at least to us, like Beckenbauer's sacrificed flesh. The details that had lain invisible in the textbook fairly burst our eardrums in person because, Schmidt and I agreed, it was the only painting we'd ever seen that *produced sound*. We felt Beckenbauer calling to us from beyond the grave, weary, lugubrious, a voice charged with anguish, but joy too, like a choir of angels, or rather, because Schmidt and I were vigorous nonbelievers, like the *equivalent* of a choir of angels, whatever the *equivalent* of a choir of angels might sound like, a symphony or an orchestra or perhaps the midair collision of two commercial aircraft. Anyway, we beheld the cliff face and the holy donkey and a sky that shook with wordless turmoil. We beheld the opulent and densely painted layers that made it clear to anyone who knew the first thing about art, painting in particular, as well as anyone with the most discerning taste, that they were undeniably gazing at a masterpiece, and without warning I wept as I had never wept before. I wept and trembled as if the world had taken on new meaning or the meaning of the world had revealed itself, I didn't know which, but anyone with a soul or a beating heart could do nothing *but* weep at the foot of *Saint Sebastian's Abyss*. And I gazed into the eyes of the holy donkey, elegiac and dim, and at the cliff face too, the painting not unlike the passage to some frontier where things were flat, time and objects both, and memories carried the soft, downy consistency of dreams, not a happy place but not a sad place either, which is something in itself, and I saw the end of the world, the barbed edge of nothingness, and it was not something to fear but to relish. Wiping my wet cheeks, I glanced at Schmidt, who seemed perturbed by my display; clicking his tongue he removed his field notebook and began taking notes. Afterward he took me to task, said that I suffered from an *oversensitivity* and this *oversensitivity* would either impede my progress as an art critic or kill any chance I had of becoming an art critic worth anything. If I wanted to become an art critic worth anything, he'd admonished, then I'd better take a good look at my soul. He told me that *Saint Sebastian's Abyss* was indeed the finest painting in existence and had replaced his favorite painting, *Minerva Victorious over Ignorance*, the moment he'd laid eyes on it. Yes, he'd declared, *Minerva Victorious over Ignorance* is now my *second favorite painting*, but the crying, he'd said, the *rigamarole* and the *fireworks*, the entire display, it's not only an embarrassment but impractical and, years later, when Schmidt was overcome by his *flood of emotions* he did the decent and the civilized thing, he boasted, which was to excuse himself. On our first visit though, tapping his temple, he'd said that a master's work should touch the mind, not the heart. Leave the heart out of it, Schmidt had said, the moment the heart is involved you're no longer a critic but a *spectator* and he'd said the word *spectator* as if it were the worst thing a person could ever be.

36

Sometimes in the Rudolf Gallery, cupping our hands to block out the two *monkey paintings*, Schmidt and I would talk about the end of the world, a subject of endless fascination for us. Cupping my hands to fend off the monstrosities of Beckenbauer's lesser works, I told Schmidt that the end of the world had fascinated me ever since childhood though I couldn't recall the impetus for the fascination. The apocalypse had always fascinated Schmidt, Schmidt explained, because the *ending* of things was all that mattered, the *ending* of things always more interesting than the beginning or the middle, for here we are at this moment, he'd said, in the middle of things and it's not very interesting, in fact it's rather tedious and boring. And the beginning, he'd declared, forget it, we'll never know the beginning because we weren't there and no one we know was there, hence it's all speculation. Removing my hands from the sides of my face I told Schmidt that the end of the world could be both seen and felt in *Saint Sebastian's Abyss* and sometimes merely walking into the Museu Nacional d'Art de Catalunya in Barcelona, knowing I would soon be face-to-face with *Saint Sebastian's Abyss*, would send my nerves aflutter for once again I would be witness to the closest approximation of the apocalypse any artist had ever rendered. The blackened cliffs that take up the lower half, I explained, and the charcoal sky rent by lightning were both telltale signs of Armageddon. And what of the holy donkey, Schmidt asked since Schmidt knew I had a soft spot for the holy donkey, knew I had strong feelings about the holy donkey, specifically the reflections in the holy donkey's eyes and, what's more, was beginning work on a book dedicated to the holy donkey, a book expressly about the symbolism of the holy donkey in *Saint Sebastian's Abyss*, which would include, of course, meditations on the reflections in the holy donkey's eyes. The donkey's eyes, I'd said, though filled with tranquility, reflect either a sky charged with devastation or the collapsing city of Jerusalem, I can't be sure which, for sometimes the donkey appears to be gazing at the sky and other times the donkey appears to be looking at the burning vista with profound regret but I see myself and all humanity in the eyes of the holy donkey, eyes saturated with meaning, charged with the burden of civilization. In either case, I continued, the reflections show a landscape entering the end-times, rapidly too, and how Beckenbauer captured and evoked such loaded reflections in the eyes of the creature is mystifying and later, sitting on the plane, approaching Berlin as well as Schmidt's deathbed, I felt sorrow for those halcyon days when we spoke without pretense about the most resplendent subjects in the world and the subjects closest to our hearts: Count Hugo Beckenbauer, *Saint Sebastian's Abyss*, and the end of the world.

37

The Rudolf Gallery was constructed in 1975 in an attempt to gather all the sixteenth-century Renaissance art donated to the Museu Nacional d'Art de Catalunya from private collections into a single space in Barcelona. Eventually it became an additional wing adjacent to the museum's extraordinary library. Devoid of natural light, it's a somber and stoic space, tasteful and unobtrusive, only steps from the famous Montjuïc fountain, and only steps, in the opposite direction, from the aforementioned extraordinary library. Schmidt and I never bothered to study the other works hanging in the Rudolf Gallery, works of religious fervor from the Low Countries, not bad of course, but not good either and correct me if I'm wrong, Schmidt would say, but if one is in the presence of the greatest artistic gesture ever made why bother turning one's head to see the mediocrity that was chosen by strangers to accompany it, art historians who obviously *respected* Count Hugo Beckenbauer and *Saint Sebastian's Abyss* but had no *feeling*, one way or the other, for either Count Hugo Beckenbauer or *Saint Sebastian's Abyss*, and the act of turning our heads, Schmidt and I unconsciously agreed, was too much of an effort, too fruitless and futile to consider and when Schmidt, on three occasions, fled from his *flood of emotions*, I doubt he ever took the time to look to his right or his left where an array of Renaissance art from the Low Countries hung and even I, bending to tie a shoe or give directions or remove a handkerchief, avoided turning my head to the right or the left to see these minor works from the Low Countries that insulted *Saint Sebastian's Abyss* merely by their proximity to *Saint Sebastian's Abyss* and without ever saying it out loud, we believed turning our heads to the right or the left, acknowledging the other works from the Low Countries in the Rudolf Gallery, was somehow analogous to admitting defeat, which was analogous to believing or accepting that art had been created *after* 1906, this never said but felt by both of us, Schmidt and I that is, a feeling intrinsically obeyed, and more than cupping our hands to the sides of our faces to block out the two lesser works, or the *monkey paintings*, was our decades-long refusal to turn our heads and look either to the right or the left in the Rudolf Gallery.

38

Schmidt and I were obsessed with not only the Northern Renaissance and Dutch Mannerism but also the Flemish school with its passion for the ideal and the sublime. Our obsession stretched to medieval art too, *especially* medieval art, because, in Schmidt's words, medieval art advocates, even declares, the triumph of death, medieval art, Schmidt would say, portrays a humanity perpetually glimpsing the apocalypse in all its sensuousness, and rightly so. Yes, he'd say, as we fled the Tudor and brick of Oxford, the lush, manicured lawns and gentle slopes, Schmidt and I taking the wooded paths near the Ruskin, walking beyond the Ruskin School to avoid our tedious Ruskin classmates, our tender hearts, that is Schmidt's and mine, bursting with love for art, the two of us reminiscing about a time when art still existed, meaning a time before 1906 or, to be more specific, any time before October 23 of 1906, since that was the date Cézanne expired from pneumonia and Schmidt would commence his breathing exercises, working his lungs by taking deep swallows of air and holding his breath for as long as possible, his thin arms outstretched and making windmills, techniques he'd picked up as a boy while taking a cure in Heringsdorf where a poet only a few years older than Schmidt at the time also resided, a poet suffering from verfolgte lunge (haunted lung), the disease in its most debilitating stages. Without making his presence known, Schmidt followed the poet during his morning constitutionals, mimicking him for weeks until he'd mastered the poet's exercises, the aggressive, almost violent exhalations, the plugging of each nostril, one at a time or in tandem, followed by a litany of bizarre coughs and other poses now happily ridiculed by our fellow students; Schmidt had a religious devotion to these breathing exercises that, he maintained, were indispensable and the only thing keeping him from death's door. The death of the poet the following season had made an enormous impression on the younger Schmidt, Schmidt holding the belief that after painters, poets possessed the most reflective and philosophical souls, meaning the most fragile lungs because the sign of a profound soul, he'd say, are troubled lungs, lungs incapable of consuming life at the rate their hearts most crave and when I meet anyone with frail lungs, he'd say, with temperamental lungs, he'd add, with lungs afflicted by the perpetual threat of collapse, I know I'm meeting a person highly attuned to the sacred and, tramping through the woods outside Oxford, I considered Schmidt's deep kinship with medieval art and the Middle Ages, in other words Schmidt's deep kinship with sickness and death because death hovered perpetually in Schmidt's life just as it hovered in the Middle Ages, an era, in Schmidt's words, rife with plagues and agony and grief, *dear God the grief,* he'd exclaim, and as a result, Schmidt would say, the Middle Ages were a period of unparalleled artistic expression because those medieval artists believed the end-times were upon them, that Satan had arrived and for any number of reasons, either for something they'd done or something they lacked, or perhaps the malicious nature of God, the end of the world was knocking on their doors and thus the greatest, most awe-inspiring paintings were created. You can't create sublime art, Schmidt would say, *eternal art,* he'd add, if you believe there will be a tomorrow and I, ambling beside him, wholeheartedly agreed. One must paint, he said, believing the Antichrist is traipsing through the next village.

39

Besides the lack of skill and technique evident in the untitled work on the left-hand side of *Saint Sebastian's Abyss* in the Rudolf Gallery in Barcelona is the mediocrity that jumps off the canvas, the overwhelming sense that the work was created by a person lacking both formal training and any sense of symmetry. A work not *flirting* with ineptitude, Schmidt would say, but *drowning* in ineptitude, as well as incomprehension and bad taste too, so much so I'm physically sickened by it, by those two monstrous *monkey paintings* that have no right to hang next to the most glorious and effulgent painting in human history and I'd love to light them on fire, both of them, and then stand and watch them burn and then celebrate, Schmidt would continue, yes, celebrate because finally *Saint Sebastian's Abyss* would be the only child it was always meant to be, not the oldest or youngest or middle child, the spurned child, the neglected child, the hapless child dragged perpetually through the gutter by his imbecilic siblings, namely the two lesser works, or the *monkey paintings*, no, Schmidt would say, the tension growing in his face, his gestures exaggerated and euphoric, eyes fixed and defiant, *Saint Sebastian's Abyss* would be the great phoenix rising, higher and more resplendent than the *Birth of Venus* or the *Mona Lisa* or even *Minerva Victorious over Ignorance*, showing the world of art what a masterwork was and then, overcome by emotion, Schmidt would plug either his right or left nostril and begin pacing in circles while flapping either his right or left arm. I too detested the *monkey paintings*, the first of the two *monkey paintings* more than the second, which, at least, had the respite of blank space in what appeared to be a failed still life, whereas the first of the two untitled works, or *monkey paintings*, assaulted the observer with near-constant aggression, the wheelbarrow and chestnut trees that seemed painted by a beginning art student with detached retinas. Schmidt, however, preferred the first of the *monkey paintings*, the one on the left-hand side of *Saint Sebastian's Abyss*, over the second because, in his words, the ugliness and horror are so brazen that one must imagine the courage it took Beckenbauer, one-handed and syphilitic, nearly blind, stumbling along the cobbled streets of Berlin or the muddy paths of Düsseldorf, attempting to sell that colossal monstrosity.

40

Flying over the Atlantic I closed my eyes and recalled the success my second wife had enjoyed with her critical biography of Paul Klee. Coupled with *that horrible thing* I'd both said and written, my second wife's success was simply too much for Schmidt. Even though Schmidt was enjoying his own success with his fourth book, *The Farmhouse,* a book examining Helga Heidel's diaries and Beckenbauer's creative peak in the Düsseldorf farmhouse where it was presumed *Saint Sebastian's Abyss* was painted, Schmidt couldn't let go of *that horrible thing* I'd both said and written, now compounded and aggravated and made decidedly worse by my second wife's critical biography of Paul Klee and the success it was enjoying and the more her book on Klee sold and the more her book on Klee was lauded and discussed the more Schmidt went out of his way to trash Klee, calling Klee unimportant and moronic, spewing vitriol about abstract art, especially cubism, calling it finger painting for blind amateurs and hacks, hacks who somehow managed to take their middle finger *while* finger painting and lift it in moronic glee toward true art and formal technique. Schmidt was so chafed by my second wife's success that his late-night calls about the apocalypse, a long-held tradition, a routine I'd come to relish and depend upon, pacing the living room in my slippers, discussing the triumph of the end-times as well as the esteem in which our beautiful books about *Saint Sebastian's Abyss* and the end-times were held, became sparse and random until eventually the phone calls ceased altogether.

41

Schmidt and I often complained about the placement of art in the Rudolf Gallery, complaints lodged in writing and as long-winded tirades directed at the officials and benefactors and endless bureaucracy of the Museu Nacional d'Art de Catalunya, though we also made sure to compliment the tasteful lighting and peerless curation of the museum as we expressed our feelings about the *crowding* of *Saint Sebastian's Abyss*. *Saint Sebastian's Abyss* is being *crowded*, Schmidt would say, in person or in a formal complaint and I would do the same. It's being *crowded* by the other paintings, I'd say, the two lesser works with their cloying gold frames, positioned equidistantly from *Saint Sebastian's Abyss* but placed *too* close and thus *crowding* the great masterwork, not letting the great masterwork breathe and simply *be* and because of this, because of the horrid placement of art, what Schmidt called the *crowding*, in the Rudolf Gallery, *Saint Sebastian's Abyss* is *suffocating*. Don't you see *Saint Sebastian's Abyss* is being *asphyxiated*, Schmidt would lament to the museum staff, sometimes taking advantage of his notorious lung condition by exaggerating his cough, which sounded like kicked gravel or a defective appliance, and due to our stature Schmidt and I were placated and humored and not once was there anything resembling a confrontation, something, I imagined, Schmidt would've relished and I envisioned him flexing his bushy mustache as he denounced the design of the Rudolf Gallery with

Beckenbauer's two monstrous works equidistant from the great masterwork and fine, yes, I could hear Schmidt saying, the paintings from the Low Countries on the opposite wall are decent, even worthwhile, but the *crowding,* the *crowding,* he'd yell, can't you see *Saint Sebastian's Abyss* is getting bullied and crowded and *suffocated,* can't you see that it's *dying*? The endless red tape that one might claim *helps* a museum operate and thrive was, in our opinion, the very red tape that *paralyzed* the Museu Nacional d'Art de Catalunya, making simple requests like having a single painting left unmolested, not *crowded* or *suffocated,* virtually impossible and because of this, because of what we called the *crowding* and *suffocating* of *Saint Sebastian's Abyss,* we always felt the work was never given the solitude and prestige that it deserved.

42

There was no debate that the centerpiece, or nucleus, of *Saint Sebastian's Abyss* was the chain of apostles floating upward toward a crepuscular sky. These apostles, painted with loving deference and unparalleled technique, received the most scrutiny in the art world and some claimed each apostle represented one of humanity's transgressions. *The Sins of Hugo's Saints* by the French critic Tristan Molyneaux, a rather listless book, Schmidt and I agreed, took this stance and Molyneaux spent dozens of pages on each apostle and the so-called *lapse in humanity* the apostle supposedly reflected. Schmidt and I detested Molyneaux and avoided Molyneaux and whenever we crossed paths with Molyneaux at various symposiums and exhibitions awash with tortuously self-satisfied art critics, not to mention their inescapable hangers-on, Schmidt went out of his way to insult Molyneaux, calling Molyneaux a fool and a dope and a simpleton. Tristan Molyneaux wouldn't even have a subject for his unreadable book if it weren't for us, I told Schmidt and Schmidt, as I'd hoped, was pleased with my insight. We're the ones who discovered Beckenbauer at the Ruskin School, I continued; if not for us and our keen eye for disregarded masters, Beckenbauer and *Saint Sebastian's Abyss* would be only a footnote in the world of art, and moreover, I'd said, Molyneaux's terrible book wouldn't exist. Schmidt again agreed and, in a rather conspiratorial tone, denounced Molyneaux's book, not even calling him a docent but a docent's *apprentice*, which was the worst imaginable indignity since Schmidt's feelings about docents were well-known and then Schmidt castigated Molyneaux's invocation of religious symbolism in *The Sins of Hugo's Saints,* truly a terrible book, Schmidt went on, the idea of involving religion in art criticism, especially of the greatest work of art in the world, *Saint Sebastian's Abyss,* is nauseating, and not because I'm an unbeliever, said Schmidt, but because I simply don't accept the notion nor the practice of God being involved in art criticism, not only when the art has nothing to do with God or religion but *especially* when the art deals with God or religion because only the artist understands, or *misunderstands,* his relationship with the false deity we call God and to write criticism about it, it being belief, is as erroneous and misguided as the belief itself. And looking askance at Molyneaux, Schmidt cursed the world of art, a world, he said, overflowing with char-latans and pigs, oafs and incompetents, who don't understand suffering and thus can't and won't understand art since they refuse to suffer and will go to the greatest lengths to avoid even the smallest whiff of suffering, although, of course, they have no problem *inflicting* suffering upon the people around them, and here Schmidt clicked his tongue in the direction of Molyneaux who, a glass of white wine in his pale hand, the face of a weasel, was laughing affably at some idiotic joke, a joke we couldn't hear but were fairly certain was idiotic, because just look at the faces of these fools, Schmidt exclaimed. It's grotesque! It's sordid! The goddamn tenants of the underworld, he whispered loudly, and disgusted, Schmidt and I liberated ourselves from the gala to have supper at Léopold's and chat about chaos, agony, and the end of the world.

43

In the symbolic center of *Saint Sebastian's Abyss* float the five apostles, varying in age, complexion, and size; the third apostle, the one in the center, is clutching a chalice in his right hand, raising it toward the bolt of lightning. This apostle, with his unusual gesture, has always received the most attention from scholars, some of whom claim the third apostle is commanding or receiving the lightning by raising the chalice, indicating he is either *touched* or *angelic* while others believe the central apostle is a stand-in for Beckenbauer himself. Had Count Hugo Beckenbauer inserted himself into *Saint Sebastian's Abyss* as the central apostle? Was *Saint Sebastian's Abyss*, with its portents of the apocalypse, its scattered bonfires, its outlandish mockery of biblical themes, a self-portrait of sorts? If so, was the purpose ironic or symbolic, allegorical or perhaps self-referential? Besides raising the chalice toward the bolt of lightning, the central apostle is the only apostle to look upward to the heavens as the others gaze in anguish at the fires below. These were the questions raised in Molyneaux's book, questions Schmidt didn't hesitate to say were beneath him and, being a strict formalist, questions he considered nonsense and ludicrously preposterous. These questions are ludicrously preposterous, he'd said, when all we have is the work itself, when what stands in front of us is the painting, nothing more, the painting itself enough to satisfy ten lifetimes of work by the greatest art critics in the world, so how can this pig and this dunce, meaning Tristan Molyneaux, write an *entire book*, meaning *The Sins of Hugo's Saints*, not an essay or even an article but an *entire book*, about what he *supposes* Beckenbauer meant? I myself was more interested in the hems of the apostles and, obviously, the holy donkey on the edge of the cliff, impervious to the turmoil beneath his hooves, what I've always considered to represent the city of Jerusalem aflame. Nestled into the cliff face one also finds serpents, braids of vines, a flaming sword, and a nest of serpent's eggs, all details of interest, though my affection for the holy donkey, the most powerful aspect of *Saint Sebastian's Abyss*, was unrivaled.

44

Because he couldn't talk about it publicly Schmidt would often call me, and later text me, about his hatred of the two lesser works, or the *monkey paintings*, how they *degraded* and *besmirched* and ultimately *poisoned* the goodwill and sanctity of *Saint Sebastian's Abyss*. Imagine if only *Saint Sebastian's Abyss* had survived, he would say, imagine if *Saint Sebastian's Abyss* was the sole surviving masterwork of Count Hugo Beckenbauer, the glowing reviews, the penetrating criticism and commentary it would've received. Already it's taken half our lives to prove its worth. Imagine how much easier it would've been had *those two pieces of shit* burned when they were supposed to, meaning, I assumed he meant, in Stockholm in 1625. Schmidt would go on in this vein, breathing heavily into the phone, Schmidt's asthmatic lungs struggling with Schmidt's growing repulsion for the two *monkey paintings*. Our life's work, he would mutter, our collective energies, he would say, all could've been spent on the worthwhile efforts of celebrating and discussing *Saint Sebastian's Abyss* instead of *proving* its worth, which, undoubtedly, would've been easy, almost too easy, *a walk in the park* as they say, if those two monstrous and repugnant works had never existed. Yes, he would go on with furious certitude, Beckenbauer's name is no doubt lauded and celebrated because of you and me, but the presence of the two lesser works precludes his name from being elevated and spoken of with the same reverence as, say, a Michelangelo or a

Vermeer or a Hendrik the Elder or, of course, a Bartholomeus Spranger. And any book I write or lecture I give, he would continue, is diluted and maimed and ultimately wasted whenever I have to include the two lesser works in any capacity because the two lesser works, the *monkey paintings*, are like uninvited guests to the ceremony of life.

45

Greatly disfigured, his left arm wholly useless, held in a sling or, conversely, dangling like a dead fin, Count Hugo Beckenbauer returned to Düsseldorf, to the Düsseldorf farmhouse, in 1540 to create an unimaginable body of work, unimaginable because all that remains is a work of staggering human complexity and sacrifice, as masterful and potent as it is small and alluring, *Saint Sebastian's Abyss*, as well as the two lesser works, as squalid as they are immense, works that would remain forever untitled and, in Schmidt's and my opinion, rightly so. Vexed by mounting debts and the small-minded patrons who pestered Beckenbauer for either the paintings they'd paid for or the return of their advance, Beckenbauer fled Berlin for a year, fled to Düsseldorf and the Düsseldorf farmhouse where even in the dreary winter when the town lay fixed in an interminable freeze, Count Hugo Beckenbauer began rapidly producing enormous canvases that reached the top of the barn's loft. Heidel writes: *I bring Hugo a bowl of coffee each morning and see the strange, otherworldly works he is making. Hugo isn't violent himself, but a violence lies beneath the surface of both the paintings and the man. If the intentions he has in his mind's eye don't match the work on the canvas he stomps in circles. Furious. Suffering. His left eye has sealed itself shut and the vision in the right is getting weaker by the day, although it still fixates on the canvas with a morbid concentration. Hugo bumps into doorways and trips on his own boots. He refuses to let me call Dr. Schröder. He has taken an old rag, drenched in oils and paint, and wrapped it around his head to cover the afflicted eye. When he has finished painting he leaves with his works and though he doesn't think I suspect it, visits the brothels where he likely sells his paintings for sexual congress for he returns without them, surly and dissipated. Some mornings I find Hugo already in the barn, engaged on a large canvas and hear the laughter of harlots from the loft above.*

46

Schmidt admired all the Early Netherlandish painters but none more than Petrus Christus whom he felt an uncommon kinship with and Schmidt would've been content devoting his entire life to studying, contemplating, and writing about Petrus Christus, especially *Portrait of a Young Girl*, but then Count Hugo Beckenbauer, in Schmidt's words, *showed up*, changing everything. Everything changed after I saw *Saint Sebastian's Abyss* he explained one day in Barcelona, outside the Museu Nacional d'Art de Catalunya, a day when Schmidt was not overcome by his *flood of emotions* but was able to stand at the foot of *Saint Sebastian's Abyss* to study and contemplate and reflect upon *Saint Sebastian's Abyss*, jotting in his field notebook and flexing his mustache, a day when the guards, with the reverence they preserved for famous scholars, cordoned off the Rudolf Gallery for the length of our stay. Afterward, beside a cluster of plane trees, Schmidt performed a breathing exercise, holding one nostril closed while standing on his left leg, an exercise called the Pelican, while he reminisced about his early love for *Portrait of a Young Girl*, the work Schmidt had planned to devote his life to in his early days at Oxford, at the Ruskin School, where we met, until we both discovered *Saint Sebastian's Abyss* in our textbook and, in his words, *the world tilted*. At the Ruskin School Schmidt raved about his two favorite paintings, *Minerva Victorious over Ignorance* and *Portrait of a Young Girl* and, eyes closed, he recreated them, reciting the details aloud, her eyes like a sphinx, he'd say, meaning the girl or subject of *Portrait of a Young Girl,* the inverted triangle of her blouse, he'd say, the opalescence and sublimity, he'd say, the transcendence of craft, he'd say, and on he would go, recreating the painting without me having to even *see* the painting and though Schmidt claimed great art criticism and art theory involved the mind, always at the exclusion of the heart, Schmidt's heart was deeply invested in art no matter what he said; each time Schmidt insisted that I leave the heart out of it I knew it was his *overabundance* of heart that frightened him, his *overabundance* of heart that plagued his conscience, his *flood of emotions* that demanded he suppress and even renounce the heart at all costs, and this contradiction or hypocrisy, I began to believe, originated from a youth in Vienna that Schmidt would mention in only the most superficial terms before quickly changing the subject, his mother and father, siblings, and grandparents never once entering the realm of conversation, merely terse allusions to a summer spent at the Mönchsberg spa, for instance, or the poet he'd once followed and mimicked now so long ago, Schmidt's youth no less cryptic, I felt, than Beckenbauer's youth hundreds of years earlier.

47

Remembering Hugo years after his death, Heidel writes: *Hugo painted with whatever materials were at hand, preferably natural ones. He loved mixing egg yolk with soil or charcoal, adding ink to create his own dyes and pigments. He did this with only the sight in his right eye. A demented fury overcame him when he painted and I, the barn, Düsseldorf, the world around him collapsed. After completing a work, despite my protests, Hugo would go in search of companionship, sometimes at Der Fuß des Hasen (The Rabbit's Foot), or Der glückliche Bär (The Happy Bear), or Freudenhaus Sehnsucht (Yearning), all the assorted brothels that lay in the grim and faithless sections of Düsseldorf. If I asked Hugo about the inspiration for his paintings he claimed mystical visions, said the hooves of the apocalypse were galloping perpetually in his brain, said he was possessed and the work itself held no interest for him, had stopped holding interest after he'd turned twenty-five or twenty-six, he couldn't remember, but he felt tired and dead inside, he confessed, and painting was not an escape, painting no longer the artistic and aesthetic calling he'd once had but something he felt compelled to do according to his visions. When he was younger he'd believed painting would bring salvation, but now it was only an itch he attempted to scratch, a demon that demanded to be exorcised every morning when he woke. Reluctantly he would eat the bowl of mush and the black bread I would place before him. And then, grabbing a walking stick he had recently whittled, he would depart to the farmhouse to paint or go in search of a villager amenable to having sex.*

48

At the Art World Conference in New York City I spoke at length about my third book, *Byzantine Dawn*, and later, on a panel, I was asked if I agreed with my great friend and colleague Schmidt in his assertion that all art after 1906 was *trash*, an opinion that had become notorious as well as fashionable as conversational currency, specifically in art circles, a seamless way of bringing up debates about art, especially art after 1906 and the question of whether it was good or *trash* and people, specifically in art circles, approached one another at galleries and exhibitions and conferences, functions all equally tedious and overrun by the petulant, asking if they agreed with Schmidt and often that was all it took, the interlocutor knowing their listener understood what it meant to *agree* or *disagree* with Schmidt, meaning what was their opinion regarding art after 1906 and did they think it was *trash*? And I on the panel, gazing at the viewers, explained in the most benevolent and generous terms that art, despite the knowledge and depth an expert brings to a specific *work* or *body of work* or, going further, an *entire movement* or, going even further than that, the *total inexhaustible breadth* of art history, is utterly and completely subjective. Art, in other words, can mean as much to the professional as to the layman, as much to the sophisticate as to the simpleton because art, when all is said and done, should touch the soul, should it not? And this answer with its warmhearted platitudes was something I'd always believed, even at Oxford, at the Ruskin School, but had simply never articulated, perhaps because the occasion hadn't presented itself or my mind hadn't formed the exact words, at least not until that panel at the Art World Conference in New York City, and my answer with its sentimental simplicity received some desultory claps and then the day moved on without me or the rest of the panel or the audience thinking anything of it. But the very next month Schmidt, bedridden in Graz with a bronchial infection, read the *transcript* of that panel in a monthly art magazine and felt betrayed and turned upon because I'd said something I'd always felt but never spoken aloud and not for any specific reason, I'd later thought, as I could've just as easily said it in front of Schmidt, in fact *to* Schmidt, and we would've likely argued as we often did, and things, meaning life, would've continued. But I didn't. I'd said it on the panel at the Art World Conference in New York City and later, after Schmidt had read the transcript of my panel at the Art World Conference in New York City where I'd said, in essence, *art is subjective* and *art is for everyone,* namely *a layman's opinion is equal to an expert's,* he divorced himself from my life, albeit slowly, incrementally, at first with insults to me and my second wife and the books we'd written, and later with slander and snubs and eventually gossip, the sort of behavior one expects from a nemesis, which, in a sense, Schmidt had (or would) become, and I imagined Schmidt reading the transcript of my panel from his bed in Graz, calling me a traitor and a defector for I had uttered *that horrible thing* without even hiding it, with me and the audience and rest of the panel hearing it and not thinking anything of it because only

Schmidt found fault with what I'd said, what I still felt was a rather plain and idealistic answer, but what Schmidt felt was *that horrible thing,* thirty or forty words at most, apparently enough to end our glorious friendship and as the plane descended over Berlin I read Schmidt's email for the umpteenth time. In it Schmidt berated me one last time, his exact words, *one last time,* for *that horrible thing* I had said and later included, if briefly, in my fourth book, *Serpent's Pastoral,* as well as my fifth, *Harlequin's Affection,* at the time still ignorant of Schmidt's contempt for my *romantic* or *democratic* view of art and yes, I had agreed with Schmidt countless times when he asserted that art had died in 1906 and I had also agreed with Schmidt countless times when he claimed that artists were an extinct species, but, in my defense, did that mean we were correct? Couldn't someone feel that art *hadn't* died in 1906, even if we felt and believed it had? Couldn't someone, however stupid and loathsome they might be, feel touched by something we deemed not art or even *trash*? We were right, of course, but wasn't there room for those who were wrong? All these questions Schmidt answered by not saying a thing and, in fact, the less he said the more he made his disapproval known until he receded entirely from my life and, unbeknownst to me, the next time I would talk to Schmidt would be on his deathbed in Berlin.

49

There lies a nothingness, a hopeless expanse that's always drawn me more to the second lesser painting than the first. Needless to say, both works are repugnant and abominable, works that, if Schmidt and I had our way, wouldn't exist. Still, the second untitled painting strikes me as a work more *at ease* with its dreary and accursed existence than *in battle* with its dreary and accursed existence. The second untitled work, or *monkey painting*, is quieter and less aggressive. The second untitled work, or *monkey painting*, allows the eyes to rest a bit. This is what I told Schmidt when he asked about my preference for the second *monkey painting* over the first *monkey painting*. The second untitled work, which hangs on the right side of *Saint Sebastian's Abyss* in the Rudolf Gallery, whose mission is apparently to make Count Hugo Beckenbauer's three remaining works a monstrous triptych of sorts, is also eight feet by twenty, enormous and encroaching, a still life that boasts a bowl of rotting fruit—pears, black grapes, plums—as well as a glass of red wine and a candle. Mosquitos in the foreground, poised along the ridge of the glass, suggest obliteration, doom, and decay, endowing the work with a theatrical quality that forces the viewer to wonder if the artist is mocking them. The plums, painted in thick, saturated brushstrokes, lie in shadow while the rest of the fruit, festering and spoiled, sits in an opaque light. Both above and below the center of the painting is an abyss, a dozen or so inches of black space and standing several yards away one wouldn't suspect there was any paint there at all, as though the bowl of fruit, the heart of the still life, had been painted on a canvas too large for it. Closer though, one sees layers of dark paint, brutal and impassioned. Schmidt termed the color *bruised charcoal*. I called it *weeping sable*, the title, in fact, of my seventh book, *Weeping Sable*, a tiny book-length essay that explores the colors used in *Saint Sebastian's Abyss* as well as the second untitled painting. The dark areas above and below the fruit are infused with mystery and are easily my favorite parts of the second *monkey painting*, since they allow the eyes to wander away from the painting itself, which is truly atrocious, giving the viewer, that is us, a reprieve from Beckenbauer's horrible attempt at a still life. I *appreciate* the blank space and *acknowledge* the blank space and, in some respects, feel *indebted* to the blank space both above and below the center of the work as it allows me to avoid the center of the work itself and reflect on other things, a meadow bathed in diaphanous light or the billowy arms of a bygone lover, or perhaps the murmuring of a winding stream, and on some occasions, moving my eyes slightly, imperceptibly to the left, I steal a glance at the unrivaled sublimity of the central painting, *Saint Sebastian's Abyss*, to give myself a jolt, a reminder that inches from the void, mere breaths from the mediocrity of the common, lies the absolution of true art.

50

The flight to Berlin was tranquil, preparing me, it seemed, for the turbulent meeting ahead, the reunion with my dearest friend, now a rival or an antagonist or, who knows, perhaps an enemy, a man whose lungs had plagued him his entire adult life and whose very coughs, like premonitions, echoed in my ears. Schmidt's email only vaguely alluded to his condition, mentioning that his days were *numbered*, that he was on his *deathbed* and felt obligated to see me one more time before the end, an end he seemed to be gloating about since he would reach the end before me, an end that obsessed us both, the end of the world, our lives, civilization, in short, the end of everything, which, he boasted, would greet him first, just as he claimed he had spotted *Saint Sebastian's Abyss* in our textbook first. He was the first at things, he wrote, and I followed. He took me to task in the email; the wretchedness and gall I had on that panel in New York, he wrote, giving amateurs and novices, *imbeciles* really, people who *hadn't* made art the primary reason for their existence like any reasonable person should, but people who saw art only as a *decoration* for their empty lives, saw art only as an *afterthought* or a subject of *minor consideration*, when art, he and I both knew, was the *only consideration*, yes, he wrote, I had given the same stature to *those monsters* in my heinous panel, he wrote, as to us, the critics, the ones who lived and breathed and practically bled for art. The email, though relatively short, went on in this vein, explaining I had failed as a critic, even when I had shown so much promise. The quintessential critic, Schmidt insisted, must be utterly objective. In order to study, contemplate, and write about a work the critic must remove *all feelings*, he wrote. Hence the *flood of emotions* had forced him to leave in those three instances, literally flee the presence of *Saint Sebastian's Abyss* whenever it, it being the *flood of emotions*, appeared, flee *Saint Sebastian's Abyss* out of *pure allegiance* to *Saint Sebastian's Abyss*, he wrote, out of dedication as an authentic critic, since he couldn't think objectively when the *flood of emotions* overtook him and if I'd stayed, he went on, if I'd tried to write in those moments, if I'd retrieved my field notebook and begun to write about *Saint Sebastian's Abyss* it would have been rubbish and false and even worse than that, a *betrayal* of art criticism and, consequently, it would have hurt *Saint Sebastian's Abyss* instead of illuminating *Saint Sebastian's Abyss*. Each time I've written about *Saint Sebastian's Abyss*, the letter continued, a letter remarkably succinct despite its nine pages, I've suppressed all the feelings and subjectivity I had. Each time I've written about *Saint Sebastian's Abyss* I've abolished my pulse, he wrote, my heartbeat, he added, and *courted death*, thus managing to see the work with pure lucidity, for the lucidity required to write great criticism, criticism faultless and unsurpassed, criticism that attempts to gain entry to the universe of art itself, means suppressing one's pulse and heartbeat, and existing in a dimension that borders on nonexistence. Always I approached *Saint Sebastian's Abyss* as an enemy of *Saint Sebastian's Abyss*, he wrote, an eternal foe of

Saint Sebastian's Abyss, and my job, as a critic, was to lay waste to the work and when the work survived, when the work was resurrected despite my attacks, when the work prevailed despite my many attempts on its life, then I had succeeded as a critic.

51

There was the time Schmidt got into an argument with my second wife about Kandinsky whom my second wife treasured and for whom Schmidt felt nothing, felt nothing for Kandinsky or Kandinsky's theories, utter indifference for Kandinsky's concepts of the *artist as prophet* and *communion with the viewer* as well as the oft-quoted passages from his book *Concerning the Spiritual in Art* in which Kandinsky, in Schmidt's words, pointlessly pontificates about the *spirit and music* of art and every theory he held on color, be it red, yellow, or mauve, in which Kandinsky, said Schmidt, waxed poetic about the *beauty and grace* of art but was, in essence, displaying the love he felt for his own authorial voice, blatantly so, and was thus not displaying a love for art but for himself. *Concerning the Spiritual in Art* was assigned to us at Oxford, at the Ruskin School, and Schmidt refused to read it and stated quite eloquently at the time that Kandinsky painted most of his works in the twentieth century, after 1906, and hence his painted works were invalid, as were, to an even greater extent, his books and opinions, a belief Schmidt held on to firmly and thirty years later, sitting across the table from my second wife, Schmidt once again expressed these feelings, word for word, all in response to my second wife's enthusiasm for Wassily Kandinsky, both his art and his books on art, specifically *Concerning the Spiritual in Art,* a work she was currently teaching, her position tenured and not without prestige, Kandinsky being an artist who touched my second wife's soul, my second wife explained, in the way only a truly great artist could, she said, by discovering the *fathomless*, the bottoms you never knew could be reached or even existed, darker and colder and vaster, more boundless than the bottom of the deepest ocean or the firmament in all its immensity, yes, she said, the celestial sphere, both the high and the low, all the notes of the human heart, and I sat mute, quite taken by my wife's high regard, even reverence, for Kandinsky, because she had always shown restraint, never possessed a flair for melodrama or grandiloquence but there she sat, beaming, glowing, utterly taken by everything Wassily Kandinsky had ever touched, talking of the universe of colors he had written about in connection with the human spirit, Kandinsky being that rare animal, she said, who touched the *quivering epicenter* of existence. And Schmidt, dabbing his mustache, told my second wife that Kandinsky was a bottom dweller. Kandinsky dwells on the bottom of modern art, said Schmidt, like a crab or some other excremental creature crawling across the bottom of the sea, ingesting everyone's shit. And my second wife, somehow expecting this, coolly finished her glass of riesling, stood, smiled, and calmly spit on Schmidt's plate. How's that for a bottom dweller? she asked, quickly terminating a dinner that was already, at least for me, an exercise in discomfort.

52

Records indicate that the summer of 1541 in Düsseldorf was miserable. The evenings, traditionally cooler, remained warm and oppressive. Practically blind, his head wrapped in a paint-soaked cloth boasting an array of colors, Count Hugo Beckenbauer walked the dusty streets, hair matted, his eyes shrouded, feeling his way with a stick. The last of his large canvases had been sold, likely for sex, and because of his limited mobility, Helga Heidel had removed the ladders from the barn to prevent *the madman,* as she now called him (not without affection), from hurting himself. Thus Beckenbauer began working on the smaller pieces that would be the last works of his life. This was the summer, according to Heidel's diaries, when Count Hugo Beckenbauer had a *sublime vision* and painted *Saint Sebastian's Abyss,* this *sublime vision* presaged by the stifling heat that clung to every inch of the everyday Düsseldorfian, leaving them dull and indolent, yet seemed somehow to animate Beckenbauer. Schmidt and I agreed that a *sublime vision* is the only way to account for the masterpiece, for even though I didn't believe in God, and Schmidt didn't believe in God, in fact we'd always taken great pride in being vigorous and committed *nonbelievers,* we always nurtured a conviction in something *other.* Hence something *other* was responsible for bestowing vision to the blind *madman* in the Düsseldorf farmhouse in the balmy summer of 1541 as he took a small canvas, no larger than twelve inches by fourteen, in fact *exactly* twelve inches by fourteen, and began etching what would later become the cliff face looking down on what we assume is Jerusalem, a cliff supporting the holy donkey whose eyes reflect a city ablaze, although no one really knows what aspects of the composition Beckenbauer painted first as there are no records and he could've just as easily begun with the bolt of lightning in the foreground, or equally the bonfires in the background, no one knows, but one evening Heidel entered the farmhouse and saw *Saint Sebastian's Abyss* on the makeshift easel, quivering in the shifting light, perfect and complete, the first human to lay eyes on *Saint Sebastian's Abyss* considering that Beckenbauer was completely blind at that point and yes, Schmidt and I maintained throughout our careers, it was a blind man who saw the infinite, yes, we'd declare, it was a blind man who depicted the hem of the apostles and the holy donkey, a blind man, we'd insist, with unparalleled talent, who'd bequeathed the title *Saint Sebastian's Abyss,* literally penned the words *Der Abgrund des Heiligen Sebastian* on the back of the canvas and yes, we'd concede, a man with a rapacious sexual appetite too, because even in his impaired state, writes Heidel, Beckenbauer, his masterwork finished, departed the Düsseldorf farmhouse to satiate his lust; in short, he sought fornication, Beckenbauer's walking stick a divining rod leading him God knows where, perhaps to Das Fell der Katze (The Cat's Fur), the nearest bordello, or Die Gähnende Hannah (Yawning Hannah) a little farther away, or Graue Maus (Gray Mouse) in the neighboring village, yet he, he being Beckenbauer, knew enough to leave the painting behind, sensing perhaps that he'd fulfilled his artistic legacy, creating a work he hadn't seen but *felt,* a work of unequivocal sublimity.

53

Several years after the panel in New York City and *that horrible thing* I'd said and later written, my second wife and I divorced. The success of her Klee biography, coupled with my despondence over Schmidt's break from our friendship, helped accelerate the decay in our marriage, a marriage that had already shown signs of wear; my disconnection, my ambivalence, my newfound solitude, all of this had me reflecting more and more about the end of the world. All he does, she'd complained to the marriage counselor, is think about the end of the world: one day it's the apocalypse and the next it's Armageddon. Isn't it delicious? I'd asked both of them, meaning my second wife and the therapist, an angular woman dressed all in beige. The end of everything, I'd said, is it not wonderful to consider? And they, meaning my second wife and the therapist, shook their heads and scowled and I realized I would soon be alone for in their faces I recognized the same expressions I'd seen growing up in my small, though not very small, town, a city really, where artistic ambitions and creative passions were seen as a touch deranged and a touch bizarre, where the arts were nice for a little escape perhaps, an afternoon diversion at most, as in, yes, let's spend an hour or two at the museum and then check it off the list, as in, what a relief, we don't need to go back again for another year and we can tell people, yes, we've been to the museum, yes, we've seen the works of art and the sculptures and those artists really were *mad*, and yes, it's nice to see and talk about art every once in a while and perhaps even *think* about it too but, of course, not for *too long* because, well, you know, it's a little *screwy,* but once a year is fine, once a year in fact is the *ideal* number of times to visit the museum, once a year and no more, and now let's get back to the business of life, so yes, in both of their expressions I saw what I'd seen growing up, namely perplexity, namely a basic misunderstanding that words would never clarify and even if my second wife had written books about art, which she had, she possessed a practical and orderly heart and was not easily swayed by passion, so yes, both of their expressions revealed to me I'd soon be alone in my very large apartment in a very expensive city, all made possible because of the books I had written about Count Hugo Beckenbauer and *Saint Sebastian's Abyss.*

54

Schmidt and I were not only atheists but proud atheists. Our nonbelief, we believed, was a superior brand of belief. And what of belief itself? As long as you had it, it being belief, what did it matter what the belief actually *was*? Although, we'd concede, the belief should certainly contain flickers of nonbelief or disbelief or, at the very least, a vigorous mistrust of blind faith. Schmidt and I believed in ink and tempera and canvas. We believed in still lifes. We believed in chiaroscuro. We believed in style and technique. We believed in Early Netherlandish painting, Dutch Mannerism, and the end of the world. Schmidt believed in Hendrik the Elder just as I believed in the holy donkey, just as neither of us believed any art had been created after 1906. We believed in art channeling what words failed and would always fail to do since human speech took the mind into account, insisted upon the human mind, which, Schmidt and I knew, was endlessly fallible. Schmidt and I both possessed functioning minds and these, we felt, helped as much as they hindered because words, borne of the mind, were slapdash and chaotic, words in fact took one only further from the soul, not closer, and the purpose of art, Schmidt and I believed, was to connect or reunite a person with their soul, to bring about a wordless communion with the infinite and thus our books, replete with endlessly fallible words, were merely attempts at approaching what painting had mastered by default, simply by excluding words.

55

The Lion Hunt by Rubens. *The Bitter Potion* by Brouwer. *The Agony in the Garden* by El Greco. Da Vinci's grotesque heads. Monsters and gargoyles. Madonnas and saints. Half tones. Shifting light. The human condition. Often inside a frame no more than a dozen inches tall, a dozen inches that transformed the soul. These were the works that intoxicated Schmidt and me at Oxford, at the Ruskin School where we met. As our classmates raved about *aesthetic expression* and *artistic empathy,* as they babbled deliriously about *abstract expressionism* or their favorite *art installation,* Schmidt and I were seeking images of saints in despair and scenic altarpieces, we were pondering the contradictory interpretations of skeletons in medieval and Renaissance painting, particularly Dutch Mannerism. Stumbling upon *Saint Sebastian's Abyss,* Schmidt and I knew, was the culmination of everything we had been searching for. The colors and shapes. The manipulation of light. The burden of mystical-religious hysteria as well as allusions to the apocalypse. The *underpainting,* I said, the *overpainting,* said Schmidt, the *play of shadows,* I said, the *dramatic illumination,* said Schmidt, and, to be fair, we were both right since *Saint Sebastian's Abyss* contained a thousand feverish contradictions and thus the more one gazed the less one knew. Years later, speaking to audiences around the world, from Copenhagen to Antwerp to Chicago, I explained it was impossible to look at *Saint Sebastian's Abyss* and see the same painting twice. Without shedding our skin, I'd say, without changing our name, seamlessly and inexplicably, we *evolve*, we become a different person every day, and so it is with *Saint Sebastian's Abyss*, one day we discern the slightest tinges of hope and the next the bottomless chasm of doom, the painting makes us recognize, as we all one day recognize, that we're at the mercy of the void, because, I'd say, *Saint Sebastian's Abyss* is the most spellbinding work of art ever produced by man and sometimes, in the later years, I'd start to cry, grateful Schmidt wasn't there yet sensing his presence, picturing his disdain, his biting words and bushy mustache, sensing Schmidt clicking his tongue in shame at my tears, narrowing his eyes in judgement, because speaking to audiences, especially in the later years, I was overcome by uncontrollable weeping, the audience under the impression it was my passion for *Saint Sebastian's Abyss* that was the catalyst for these emotional tantrums and not the absence of Schmidt or my second wife, the crowd not suspecting it was the isolation and loneliness and weeklong bouts of despair that had begun pervading my life.

56

From Heidel's journals: *A great storm shook the village last night. I awoke to pounding at the door. It was Hugo, drenched and raving. The bandage that covered his eyes had fallen, slipped around his neck like a kerchief, and his eyes resembled two grapes that had been left on the vine too long. He was holding a large knife and I wasn't scared for myself as much as I was scared for him. Why was he holding a knife? Where had he gotten it? Why was it so large? These were questions I wanted to ask but he was agitated, talking incessantly about the great deluge that would swallow all of us, a biblical flood, he swore, a great deluge, an apocalypse. A thunderstorm must be a frightening thing for someone without sight. Outside the cows and sheep were unsettled. This was a tremendous storm, a cacophony really, the most violent the region has seen in decades. I made him sit in the kitchen and warm himself by the stove but I asked him for the knife first, which, distracted, unsettled, continuing to exclaim about the great deluge, he handed to me absentmindedly. But he wouldn't relax, he kept repeating the deluge, the deluge, the great deluge. He wouldn't stop talking about the great deluge and the end of the world.* Reading Heidel's journals only enforced the kinship Schmidt and I felt for Beckenbauer; our shared fixation on the apocalypse or, in Beckenbauer's own words, *the great deluge*, was the sign of a deep and reflective soul. How can one live and exist, we'd pondered, but not obsess over death? How can one be alive and not be enraptured by death? It seemed impossible. We adored Beckenbauer because in Beckenbauer we saw ourselves: agitated, a head full of bats, peals of laughter, bursts of color at the very least, yes, a blind head bursting with color. In our minds, it was hardly possible to contemplate any subject *but* the apocalypse. There's resurrection or rebirth, said Schmidt, if you happen to believe in *that utter bullshit.* But to us resurrection, or, for that matter, the afterlife, was a fairy tale. We were enthralled by the end of the world, or *the great deluge,* and little else because it was the unadorned truth and Schmidt would berate anyone who suggested it was impossible to think solely of death because they were turning away from the unadorned truth, and those who claimed a person must consider both sides, consider rebirth as well as the apocalypse, Schmidt would rebuke with disgust, explaining vehemently that a person *didn't* have to consider *both sides* because perhaps, just perhaps, there weren't two sides at all, although, he'd add, if one were raised on trash and saccharin, if one were, for example, raised in the land of vapid lunacy that is the United States, then one would never realize that more often than not there is indeed *only one side,* that side being, by its very nature, the unadorned truth, not the *happy* and the *tidy* and the *inexplicably good,* no, but the tedious and the odious, the insipid banality of existence, day after day slinking toward death or, likewise, standing perfectly still and observing death's covert advance *toward you,* it doesn't matter. The belief in happy endings, he'd continue, is the biggest disservice humanity has done to itself in the history of the world for this belief was concocted purely to delude, to turn one's eyes away from the unadorned truth and Count Hugo Beckenbauer saw the unadorned truth, he'd conclude, and it had left him blind.

57

I decided to visit Spain for a month, Barcelona to be specific, the Rudolf Gallery in the Museu Nacional d'Art de Catalunya to be more specific than that. One day I came upon Schmidt, alone like me, gazing at the monstrous triptych, in other words *Saint Sebastian's Abyss* and the two lesser works, and as expected, Schmidt had both hands cupped to the sides of his face in order to block out the atrocities that are the *monkey paintings*. I studied Schmidt, his back slumped, the field notebook at his feet. Schmidt had gotten older; I saw a cane nearby, presumed it was his, and suddenly realized how much time had gone by, meaning, of course, how much the time remaining in our lives had diminished. In the slump of his back I saw the future that awaits all of us, the quiet hesitation in each gesture, the foot gingerly tapping the floor in advance, testing the ground like water in a bath, making sure the floor, and thus the earth, was stable. Schmidt was only two years my senior but the ailments he'd long suffered had accelerated his aging and if I saw the end of the world in *Saint Sebastian's Abyss* I saw my own mortality in Schmidt's hunched frame, the brittle shadow that quivered along the floor like a small bird. We hadn't spoken in years, perhaps a decade, and I cursed the cruel terror of time, a soft, indiscernible whisper that nonetheless ravages everything, forests and cities, mountain ranges, entire histories, simply by doing what it was designed to do, which is waiting, because time's only job is to exist, to wait on nothing but itself, and poor antiquated Schmidt, bending down for the field notebook, sluggish and spent, resembling an octogenarian, startled me beyond words and I fled in horror from the Museu Nacional d'Art de Catalunya and a day later fled Barcelona altogether. Instead of approaching Schmidt and asking Schmidt for Schmidt's forgiveness I flew back to the expensive city where I lived, to my very large and very empty apartment, and, unbeknownst to me, I wouldn't see Schmidt again until I visited Schmidt on his deathbed in Berlin.

58

My sixth book, *Hugo's Paradox*, was an exploration of what
Count Hugo Beckenbauer's other paintings *probably* looked
like. Based on Helga Heidel's diaries and the two *monkey
paintings* as well as the research Schmidt and I had con-
ducted before I'd said *that horrible thing* (and thus before our
falling-out), I conceptualized the body of work that was lost
in the great fire. These were portraits of various Düsseldorf
and Berlin prostitutes, I deduced, all of them small works, of
course, due to Beckenbauer's blindness, but works of solace
and redemption; I envisioned the liquid eyes of those desti-
tute harlots, the abundant tangles of black hair, the remote
expressions of those ancient faces, I saw it all and the world
of art celebrated *Hugo's Paradox* as a work of peerless and
original speculative art criticism. Schmidt responded with
a book of critical essays (*Turbulent Incoherence*) tearing apart
every theory and postulation I'd made in *Hugo's Paradox*.
Schmidt asserted that Beckenbauer's other paintings were
insipid and petulant, basing his arguments on the accounts
of those who knew him in Düsseldorf and Berlin, in addition to Helga Heidel's diaries, which described an acutely
deranged Beckenbauer raving at children and animals as well
as defecating in public, taking great joy, in fact, in defecating in public and thus his later works, Schmidt concluded,
were not only cloying and odious but affronts to art. Thus,
it seemed, a war had begun: each book Schmidt wrote about

Saint Sebastian's Abyss was a response to a book *I* had written about *Saint Sebastian's Abyss,* or the other way around, I can't remember anymore, but our books became attacks and insults, books like accusations and books like warfare. I wrote another book, *Still Life with Lucifer,* exploring the use of hell and its motifs in *Saint Sebastian's Abyss;* Schmidt responded with *Sullied Kingdom,* a book exploring the use of heaven and its motifs in *Saint Sebastian's Abyss.* Sides were chosen since critics of art and students of art couldn't be on both sides at once. Like anything in the world, a stance was required. The world of art, Schmidt once said, especially art criticism, he'd added, was a knife fight, it was warfare and carnage, and it appeared our blades had been unsheathed. Quite quickly I gained disciples and Schmidt gained disciples, students and critics and collectors of art who hung on our every word and studied our books almost religiously, and these disciples fought doggedly to defend our works, Schmidt's or mine, depending on the faction, and attacked the works of the opposing side with great ferocity. Schmidt's disciples often appeared at my lectures to harangue and disparage. My disciples, likewise, began to appear at Schmidt's lectures to harangue and disparage, although Schmidt made fewer and fewer public appearances due to his various ailments. Still, there was no question Schmidt was paying close attention to my academic work; I wrote an article about the *distortion of scope* in *Saint Sebastian's Abyss* and not three weeks later Schmidt published an article about the *adherence to scope* in *Saint Sebastian's Abyss.* I delved into the *fantastic* and *dreamlike* interpretations of Count Hugo Beckenbauer and Schmidt delved into the *plausible* and *realistic* interpretations of Count Hugo Beckenbauer, invoking the Romantic masters Géricault and Delacroix in an attempt, it seemed, to embolden his disciples, who, indeed, felt emboldened to interrupt my most well-attended speeches, some having grown mustaches out of respect and reverence for Schmidt whose woolly mustache was one of the most notorious aspects of one of the two great *Beckenbauerian* scholars in the world, I being the other, and these disciples of Schmidt didn't stand on ceremony but heckled and harassed until speaking on panels and attending conferences no longer held any interest for me and, like Schmidt, I felt obliged to go into hiding, although to a much lesser extent.

59

There exist three accounts of Count Hugo Beckenbauer's offers to paint portraits in exchange for intercourse during his final days in Berlin. With death slouching toward his door, Beckenbauer's urge for carnal relations didn't decrease but flourished, and judging from the reports that survive, the more incapacitated Beckenbauer became, the more eager he was for sexual congress. One story stands out: a Dominican friar traveling through the Rhineland on his way to Burgundy to serve at the Abbaye de Cluny stopped overnight in Berlin to visit his brother. Peter der Sachse, the Teutonic, left a record that was recently discovered in the Berlin archives and describes a man who I can only assume was Count Hugo Beckenbauer. *A strange blind man,* it reads, *feels his way by stick down Stralauer Straße, accosts citizens and vendors in order to find the local brothel, Das Fell Der Katze (The Cat's Fur), and is chased out almost as soon as he arrives, his gaunt skull bandaged in what seems to be a rag dipped in pigments and oils. My brother witnessed this poor man fumbling for his walking stick because the harlots had robbed him of the stick as a joke after he had offended them. This strange man, my brother says, known throughout Berlin, had offered to paint portraits of the harlots if he could have his way and they were outraged by the suggestion.* Not much later a young strumpet with a rare taste for art agreed to have her portrait painted by Beckenbauer in exchange for intercourse, and the resulting painting, hanging in her granddaughter's apartment sixty years later, was espied by a traveling Swedish art collector who, fascinated and beguiled by the work, offered the young woman, who was also a prostitute, a small fortune in exchange for the portrait and any information she had about its creator. It was a sizable sum, which the granddaughter of the initial strumpet accepted (the women in this family were exceptionally adroit regarding the commerce of sexual relations and thus whoring, like the portrait, was ostensibly an heirloom). The aforementioned sizable sum was paid by the Swedish art collector to the strumpet's granddaughter, a strumpet herself, to tell him everything she knew about the artist who had painted her grandmother's portrait all those years ago and though the story was vague and contained various contradictions, the Swedish art collector gleaned enough information to explore Berlin and, later, Düsseldorf, buying and collecting everything Count Hugo Beckenbauer had painted in his short, tragic life, a dozen or more portraits of sixteenth-century prostitutes, a pair of enormous still lifes, and a small painting, only twelve inches by fourteen, titled *Saint Sebastian's Abyss.*

60

There were my disciples and there were Schmidt's disciples
and both were at war and sometimes I read articles that
detailed the hostilities between these two camps, camps I
felt detached and far removed from and I assumed it was the
same for Schmidt, meaning Schmidt too felt detached and far
removed from his followers, because Schmidt had stopped
making public appearances, in fact Schmidt had become a
recluse of sorts, hiding in Vienna, still writing books about
Saint Sebastian's Abyss but no longer sitting down for interviews or attending conferences or panels, just living as a
recluse in Austria, writing books about *Saint Sebastian's Abyss*
that often felt like attacks on my books about *Saint Sebastian's
Abyss.* Sometimes I'd walk the streets of my expensive city
and find myself harassed by nascent thugs whom I recognized
immediately as Schmidt's disciples, at first by the way they
advanced with their thick defiant mustaches, grown in honor
of Schmidt, but also by the way they stopped me to curse my
body of work, indeed my entire career, calling me a traitor and
an imposter, and the lady who accompanied me, the obvious rebound from my second wife, would stand back, mouth
agape, as these bushy-mustached goons insulted my theories,
going so far as to say I hadn't even been in the classroom at
Oxford, at the Ruskin School, when Schmidt had famously
discovered *Saint Sebastian's Abyss,* something we all knew was
ludicrous and a lie, a complete fiction, and inside I wept, for

I was exasperated and exhausted by the lengths Schmidt's disciples would go to sully me, meaning to elevate Schmidt, because I too had grown tired, too tired really, to fight back with words or facts, much too occupied with the end of the world and my current relationship, an obvious rebound from my second marriage, to consider Schmidt's disciples or even the critics and connoisseurs who pestered me unceasingly about Schmidt and Count Hugo Beckenbauer and *Saint Sebastian's Abyss* and in my opinion, they'd demand, who was winning? It was all too much and when the disciples from my camp, following me in droves, books clutched in their hands, pleaded to hear my plans for the next *assault* or *attack*, meaning the next book or article I planned to write, I wanted to hurl insults, I wanted to destroy them all, because what I wanted more than anything was to be standing *beside* Schmidt, *in concert* with Schmidt, at the foot of *Saint Sebastian's Abyss* along with Schmidt, hands cupped to the sides of our faces, debating art, transcendence, and the glory of apocalypse.

61

Wilhelm Franz Günther, I'd suggested, a name chosen out of thin air. *Wolfgang Friedrich Groß,* Schmidt had suggested, both of us pointlessly hoping to endow with meaning the initials in the lower-left corner of *Saint Sebastian's Abyss,* the WFG etched into the cliff face, in many ways the most mysterious aspect of the painting, the aspect most debated and investigated and not only by us but also, later, by the younger art historians, a generation behind us, half of them followers of Schmidt and the other half followers of mine, and neither camp could find the meaning behind the dedication, the rationale behind those letters an eternal riddle that eluded the most disciplined of scholars. There they sat, three blatant, highly legible letters, with no explanation. Studying the pages of Helga Heidel's diaries, scouring the archives in both Düsseldorf and Berlin, performing name searches, swapping titles with places, places with titles, none of it amounted to anything. Schmidt and I had been to countless museums, visited the historical societies and records offices in both Berlin and Düsseldorf, and even gone to Lisbon where a private art school had been established to study Beckenbauer's three existing works since no one in the world appreciates Beckenbauer like the Portuguese, the people of Lisbon especially, where Beckenbauer is as close to a celebrity as an artist could ever hope to be. We'd scoured the private papers and accounts of the era and come up with nothing. We visited

Stockholm, but still nothing. Was it a dedication? The name of a friend? A mentor? A prostitute Beckenbauer had been enamored of? Being the most famous and celebrated Beckenbauer scholars in the world, we were asked this question most often and after our falling-out due to *that horrible thing* I'd both said and written, I would often, at conferences and panels, even in interviews, embellish what *I thought* the initials stood for, always assuring the listeners that I was merely being playful, that these were half-baked theories at best because, at the end of the day, no one could discover what the letters WFG stood for and an idiot's guess was as good as anyone's.

62

We coursed through the Berlin night, the taxi taking me along Müllerstraße, crossing Luxemburger and Triftstraße. I trembled as I felt myself getting closer to Schmidt and Schmidt's deathbed, though I wouldn't visit Schmidt on his deathbed until the next day. Fear pulsed through my limbs. Troubled, restless, I folded and unfolded Schmidt's relatively short email. I considered all nine pages of Schmidt's rather succinct dispatch, which was not an apology or a gesture of reconciliation but a recapitulation of all his past grievances. Resolute and steadfast, Schmidt insulted my books and my theories on *Saint Sebastian's Abyss*. Schmidt insulted the holy donkey and my second wife's critical biography of Paul Klee. He again insisted he was the one to turn the page first in the textbook at the Ruskin School, coming upon Count Hugo Beckenbauer's painting before I did. Not a huge discrepancy, he wrote (as he had enough faith in me to believe that had I turned the page first I would've undoubtedly noticed and recognized the work for what it was), but still, he wrote, he found it deeply unsettling that I'd always craved the credit, and also, what of *that horrible thing* I had said on that panel in New York? What the fuck was that about? It put everything into question, he wrote, everything I had ever said or done or written, and not only about Count Hugo Beckenbauer and *Saint Sebastian's Abyss* but about art itself and friendship and technique as well as shadows and shifting light, doom and decay, really *everything* we'd ever cared about. And how, he'd asked in the email, could he ever trust his best friend when his best friend had uttered and later written the words of a complete stranger, a stranger evidently suffering from dementia or a mental disability, perhaps the words of a lowbrow or an ignoramus or a person who'd been struck on the head by a piece of wood or a metal pipe, yes, he'd written, a metal pipe, not quite unconscious but *teetering* toward unconsciousness, the blow was struck and there I was, a celebrated critic, blathering idiotically about the *democracy* of art criticism, how? Had everything been a farce, he'd demanded in his email, had everything been a falsehood, a fiction, were the past three decades, he'd asked, a *fucking fabrication*?

63

Schmidt and I were often asked *why*. Why *Saint Sebastian's Abyss*? Our bodies of work—the speeches, the books, the book-length essays—speak for themselves, we'd answer. But who can deny the fusion of high and low? The motifs of ecstatic grandeur— apostles, the fall of man, rebirth—mixed with the insignificant? The eloquent blended with the banal, the lavish embroidered to the common? *Saint Sebastian's Abyss* suggests a soul at war with itself, a soul desperate to believe in the works of God but living in a world that showed no evidence of them. Consider the torrid conflict between the strokes, we'd say. Consider the lines that enclose the drama, we'd also say, giving the viewer an almost instant sense of claustrophobia. The vines along the cliff face, which suggest naturalism, wreathed around a flaming sword, which portends the abstract. Who, we'd ask, *couldn't* love and revere *Saint Sebastian's Abyss*? Schmidt might say *technique*. I might say *physicality*. Schmidt might say *perspective*. I might say *shadow*. Schmidt might say *anxiety*. I might say *despair*. The reasons, of course, were endless, and it was impossible to consider my life without *Saint Sebastian's Abyss* and even more impossible to consider my life before *Saint Sebastian's Abyss*, the days before Oxford and the Ruskin School, before meeting Schmidt, all a collection of dull and uninspired hours; looking back, I saw my youth as a vacant expanse, a desert of recurring days without light or hope, an existence given life and promise only by the *possibility* of Count Hugo Beckenbauer and *Saint Sebastian's Abyss*.

64

Little is known of Count Hugo Beckenbauer's years as an apprentice in Berlin. He lived someplace. He ate food. He survived. But something disruptive happened, some cataclysmic event around his twentieth year, prompting an inner war between belief and nonbelief, between the physical world and the spiritual, and though we can never know Beckenbauer's inner life, hints abound in *Saint Sebastian's Abyss*, and my tenth book, *The Assemblage*, explored this evidence with vigilant meticulousness. During the writing of *The Assemblage* I hid away from the world, joined by my girlfriend, the obvious rebound from my second wife, who didn't mind my obsession with the end of the world but saw it instead as a charming foible, harmless but crucial for my work. I put aside the noise and clamor of Schmidt's disciples, who had grown in number (as well as in the viciousness of their attacks) and I avoided the reverence and adoration of my own disciples in order to devote myself wholeheartedly to Count Hugo Beckenbauer and the writing of *The Assemblage*. Sporadically I'd hear murmurs from the world of art about Schmidt: how Schmidt had sold his deceased parents' Viennese home and relocated to Berlin; how Schmidt was writing his last book on Beckenbauer, which would be the *final word* on *Saint Sebastian's Abyss;* that his various diseases had gotten the upper hand and Schmidt had retreated to Berlin where he would write his *final book*, which would be, he'd claimed, the *final word* on *Saint*

Sebastian's Abyss; and that he would then retire because after this book, Schmidt had apparently declared, nothing would remain to be said. And I waited and Schmidt's disciples waited and the entire world of art, I think, waited for Schmidt's *final word* on Count Hugo Beckenbauer and *Saint Sebastian's Abyss* because who could know what it would entail?

65

On the evening of September 1, 1625, a fire broke out in Stockholm, in the neighborhood of Stadsholmen to be more specific, and on Kåkbrinken street to be more specific than that. The Swedish art collector, who had spent the last decade traveling Europe, collecting art and cheating on his wife, was not home when the fire, which lasted three days, swept through the city, killing his family and destroying his vast collection of both Renaissance and Dutch masters. The Great Stockholm Fire raged for three days and forever changed the layout of the Stadsholmen neighborhood; it also led to the creation of stricter fire codes for a city that had been spared wars, plagues, and famines but never fires. Alerted to the misfortune, the Swedish art collector raced home from Basel where he'd gone to buy art and possibly cheat on his wife. The only room in his home that had partially survived held his collection of obscure European artists, mostly from the previous century, a muddled collection of eccentric unknowns for whom the collector felt a strange affection. Included in this collection was a series of portraits, mostly of pox-ridden prostitutes; unfortunately these portraits were destroyed. Though the scene was never described, I always envisioned the collector jumping down from the carriage, utterly bereft, bemoaning the ashes of his life, now gone, gazing upon the charred remains, weeping over the loss of his loved ones, his estate, his collection of old masters, any number of things.

And I envisioned the collector regarding the one room that partially remained, a bulk of the roof destroyed, a ray of light splitting the clouds like the rod of divinity and illuminating Beckenbauer's three surviving paintings, the two lesser works and *Saint Sebastian's Abyss*, and I imagined the Swedish collector, like Schmidt and me centuries later, consecrating these works, convinced some celestial body deemed they were worthy of being spared and though I'm a proud unbeliever like Schmidt, the one true religion, in our eyes, being unbelief itself, or if not unbelief then art, yes, art was our religion, I still found solace in this story wholly fabricated by my own imagination. Call it a celestial cloud or a star, a greater being saying, in essence: *I have salvaged the greatest painting in human history along with two grotesque works to instruct you on contrast, to show humankind what is and isn't art.* Nothing more is known of the Swedish art collector except shortly after the fire he donated Beckenbauer's works to the Livrustkammaren and disappeared into the vortex of history.

66

Sequestered in my expensive apartment I paced and pondered, fretting about the release of my next book, *The Assemblage*, and whether it should be before or after the release of Schmidt's next book because if Schmidt's next book was, as he claimed, the *final word* on Count Hugo Beckenbauer and *Saint Sebastian's Abyss*, then where would my next book, *The Assemblage*, stand? And I looked out the windows of my expensive apartment at the expensive city below, not only an expensive city but a *prohibitively* expensive city, a city filled with millions of souls living their lives, oblivious to art, oblivious to doom and decay, a million weary souls indifferent to the apocalypse, crossing streets, getting in and out of cars, trading in joy and grief, discontent and despair, the endless emotions to which we're all invariably prone, none of them giving a shit about art, none of them knowing, in fact, the first thing about Count Hugo Beckenbauer or *Saint Sebastian's Abyss* and I considered calling my editor, asking if I should have *The Assemblage* published sooner or later, meaning before or after Schmidt's book, what Schmidt called the *final word* on *Saint Sebastian's Abyss*, because I didn't know if Schmidt's *final word* would indeed be the *final word* or merely a way of drawing me out because each of our books had become an attack, a response, each one more virulent and personal then the last and I no longer remembered whose turn it was to retreat or attack even though our acolytes knew full well the score for there were symposiums awash with our disciples, meaning mine and Schmidt's, who had no qualms about debating and arguing and fighting, frequently and doggedly, in order to claim victory in our names. Meanwhile my girlfriend, the obvious rebound from my second wife, scoured the art magazines for gossip and hearsay regarding my and Schmidt's disciples, meaning the articles written by our disciples against one another—arguments about technique over emotion or the implausibly aloof expression in the holy donkey's eyes and was it sanguine or tragic?—and I heard her cackles from the other room as I perspired and obsessed over the assembling of my book *The Assemblage*, and were the chapters in the correct order, I'd ask myself, were the chapters ordered to benefit my argument, namely the greatest possible configuration to deflect any arrows of criticism shot by Schmidt and Schmidt's faction? And meanwhile the obvious rebound from my second wife was shrieking, insisting I come out. You have to read this, she'd cry, or, *Jesus*, the balls on these assholes, meaning Schmidt's followers, and the more she insisted I pay attention to the outward affairs of our factions, meaning Schmidt's and mine, the more I shut myself in, the deeper I cocooned. Sometimes, to quell my anxieties, I'd dream of jumping out of the window of my expensive apartment and crashing upon the sidewalk of my very expensive city, bones crushed, everything black. No more books. No more paintings. No more books *about* paintings. No more rebound from my second wife, who didn't love or even like art, who admired, at most, only the *idea* of art, who enjoyed the scandals and rumors that fluttered around art like mosquitoes around carrion, picking the meat and bones from art until nothing resembling art was left. No more anything ever again, I'd muse, a nothingness like the brush-strokes of dark plum both above and below the center of the second *monkey painting*, a blackness so dark it was cosmic and never-ending.

67

The aesthetics of the second *monkey painting* suggest that even Beckenbauer knew he'd gone too far with the brash hideousness of the first *monkey painting* since there is a restraint and tranquility in the second *monkey painting* that isn't found in the first *monkey painting* where liberties are taken and failed experiments abound. Despite the first *monkey painting* being Schmidt's choice of the two, we shared an equal loathing for both lesser works and while we were celebrated throughout the world of art for our discovery of Count Hugo Beckenbauer, Schmidt and I lectured with an almost pathological resentment toward the *monkey paintings*, a resentment bordering on abhorrence, because all we wanted, naturally, was to talk about *Saint Sebastian's Abyss*. And in those early years I visited Schmidt in Austria and Schmidt, likewise, visited me in the United States, even though he called the United States *an exercise in the ludicrous* or *an obese infant with a head injury* and Schmidt became acquainted with my first wife whom he despised and later my second wife whom he despised even more and at dinners and receptions Schmidt would attack my first and later my second wife, their opinions about art and art theory, and the ensuing arguments would last for hours. My second wife was well equipped for these attacks, however, as she was not only versed in art and art history but was a professor and scholar herself and I would watch as Schmidt flexed his mustache, jeering at my second wife's taste, describing all modern art as derivative of real art, meaning it was *trash*, calling my second wife's line of work *the forensics of garbage* and my second wife would laugh, a shrill laugh, an utterly distinct laugh, a laugh I happened to find endearing but Schmidt must've found petulant because he wasn't used to being laughed at, not in Europe and certainly not in the United States and by an American no less. One particular evening, for instance, Schmidt explained that Count Hugo Beckenbauer's utter indifference to royalty and kings in his three surviving works was brave and progressive for an artist essentially from the sticks—this was a conversation over dinner, at a gloomy restaurant in Belgrade, the three of us out for a meal following a symposium about the dilemma of aesthetics or the turmoil of mysticism or perhaps the false guise of abstract art, I forget—and my second wife laughed at Schmidt and Schmidt asked what she'd found so amusing, making my second wife laugh even more, practically losing herself, gripping the table's edge as tears rolled down her cheeks and again he asked, demanded, to know what she, my second wife, found so goddamn hilarious and then she did indeed lose herself, and I sat there in the middle, wanting it to stop, and my second wife, guffawing, weeping copiously, was incapable of stopping, diners glancing over, my second wife pressing the napkin to her eyes, shoulders shaking, her laughter not only *not* subsiding but *growing*, Schmidt and I both ignorant of its cause, and the more Schmidt asked the harder my second wife laughed and the fact that she would never supply Schmidt with an answer, in fact *refused* to supply Schmidt with an answer as to what she found so funny, coupled with the success of her Klee biography, was more than Schmidt could take and later, in the hotel, when I insisted she tell me what she had found so funny my second wife, as if it were the most obvious thing in the world, shouted, *Him! Him!* He's an absurd man, she'd said, and the more serious he is the more absurd he becomes. And deep inside I felt she was expressing her opinion of both Schmidt *and me*, that this was her assessment of her husband after eight years of marriage, eight years of me siding with Schmidt and exalting Schmidt and believing that the art we, meaning Schmidt and I, cared about was more important and lofty than the art she cared about. At any rate, it was more than Schmidt could abide, being laughed at, and the next time we saw one another he said my second wife, in his eyes at least, was dead, which, in earlier days, I would've protested, but she and I were in therapy by then, she deeply unhappy and I talking incessantly about the holy donkey and the end of the world, quite often both, and thus we weren't doing well, our marriage I mean, and the energy required to defend her was either too difficult to muster or not there at all.

68

I'd shelved my book on the holy donkey and written instead *The Assemblage* because, in truth, it unnerved me to think about completing my book on the holy donkey, actually putting the finishing touches on my holy donkey book because of Schmidt and Schmidt's followers and the inevitable attacks that would occur once it was published, attacks not only against me but against the holy donkey as well as my holy donkey book and this was too terrifying to consider since the holy donkey was easily my favorite detail of *Saint Sebastian's Abyss* but also, I felt, the most imperishable aspect of *Saint Sebastian's Abyss*, the most innocent and enduring, and an attack against me I could take, something I'd already proven, but I hadn't the fortitude to endure attacks against the holy donkey and my holy donkey book and hadn't the holy donkey suffered enough, I'd ask myself aloud in my study, hadn't the holy donkey witnessed the burning of Jerusalem, I'd also ask myself aloud in my study as I surrendered completion of my holy donkey book, in fact *shelved* my holy donkey book out of trepidation and fear in order to write *The Assemblage* instead? And what, I'd ask myself, also aloud in my study, is an art critic who is afraid? What is an art critic who skirts around angst and doubt, censoring and sanitizing themself rather than speaking their mind? An art critic governed by fear is impotent, I'd answer myself, also aloud in my study, yes, I'd repeat, but this time more softly, yes, that art critic is barren and defeated and may as well, as the expression goes, *hang up their hat* because that art critic is no longer an art critic but a husk of their former self, and lastly I'd tell myself, once again aloud in my study, it might very well be time to hang up my own hat because I was no longer myself, no longer the brash and brave authority I'd been in my youth, but a critic afraid of criticism, a critic living in fear of ridicule, about me, certainly, but equally afraid of ridicule for the book I had shelved about the holy donkey.

69

The Brandenstach, a tasteful building in the Wilhelmine style
with nothing to suggest that my former best friend and
ex-spiritual guide as well as ex-confidant in art and art history lay dying within the confines of its walls, stood innocu-
ously along Reichenberger Straße in the center of Kreuzberg.
Good, I told myself, *this building, the Brandenstach, with its
historical motifs and tasteful composition, looks exactly like the
building I imagined Schmidt would choose to face his own death
in.* Before calling for the taxi I read and reread the email, all
nine pages creased from incessant folding and unfolding, the
urgent underlining during the flight, each word emblazoned
upon my mind, Schmidt's vitriol and fury hard to reconcile
with the man I envisioned approaching the abyss, his relent-
less and intractable hatred for *that horrible thing* still undimin-
ished years after I'd both said and written it, his myopic focus
on what art is and what art isn't, as well as who is allowed
to decide, still the topic that most rankled his soul. I arrived
at the Brandenstach a little before noon and asked the driver
to wait; I peered from the taxi's back seat, on the lookout for
any of Schmidt's disciples, those feverish acolytes who lived
all over the world and wouldn't hesitate to fly wherever they
were needed to help their cause, which, in essence, was ele-
vating Schmidt and bolstering Schmidt, and thus maligning
me; I gazed through the rear window for the slightest trace of
Schmidt's zealots, all of them eager to stir up trouble by calling

me a coward, a phony, and an *enemy of art.* I was concerned word had somehow reached them of my arrival in Berlin, my visit to see Schmidt on his deathbed, though I was confident I would discover their presence quite quickly because, firstly, the mustaches grown in honor of Schmidt were blatant, and secondly, they had an unmistakable and urgent way of charging toward me with either *August in Rhapsody* (Schmidt's first book) or *Sullied Kingdom* (Schmidt's eighth book) grasped in their agitated hands, although, to be honest, it could just as easily have been any of Schmidt's various books, his second as much as his fourth, his fifth as well as his sixth, for I had seen these sycophants at different instances holding different titles, some containing prefaces or addendums by yours truly, though Schmidt's first and eighth books were unfailingly the tomes most prominent and hence the most frequently held aloft. Grudgingly I'd learned the names of some of Schmidt's most ardent disciples, not because I'd wanted to but because the obvious rebound from my second wife loved nothing more than reading aloud articles about our so-called *hostilities,* frequently summoning me to the living room to highlight an especially amusing insult, and always in the background of our home was the sound of the television (the obvious rebound from my second wife *adored* television) and I would hear our disciples, mine and Schmidt's, arguing on panels or being interviewed about whose side—Schmidt's or mine—they were on and why, and often Tristan Molyneaux's voice would emerge since he was undoubtedly the third most important Beckenbauerian scholar after Schmidt and me and he'd obviously been asked to appear as a guest on some moronic but specifically art-focused program and Molyneaux, of course, couldn't help himself and was invariably asked what was his opinion of the *hostilities* between me and Schmidt, Molyneaux siding with me for one book and Schmidt for the other, depending on the climate at the time and who happened to be in favor; Molyneaux moralizing, pontificating, expressing *his profound disappointment* and *utter heartbreak* over my and Schmidt's falling-out and our current *hostilities*, when nothing, I knew, could've made him happier. One afternoon the obvious rebound from my second wife blurted, *it's being televised from Lisbon,* meaning the panel or conference or symposium she was watching, not realizing that Portugal was the home of the most fervent and loyal fans of Count Hugo Beckenbauer's art in the world, that even before Spain and Poland, the Portuguese *revered* Count Hugo Beckenbauer and his three surviving works more than anyone else and each October a parade in honor of Beckenbauer's three surviving works wound its way through the steep and sinuous streets of Old Lisbon with children dressed as the serpent or the apostles or even the holy donkey, fireworks illuminating the inky sky, brass bands playing, and bottles of *Vinho Verde* being drunk without restraint, and despite Beckenbauer's works hanging in Barcelona, in the Museu Nacional d'Art de Catalunya to be more specific, in the Rudolf Gallery to be more specific than that, the Portuguese adored *Saint Sebastian's Abyss* and the two lesser works and it wasn't uncommon to find both cheap and rather expensive reproductions of Beckenbauer's works adorning the living rooms of the middle and upper-middle class of Lisbon specifically, but also the rest of Portugal and she, not understanding any of this, because the rebound from my second wife was both lazy and incapable of understanding that Portugal was, in fact, the country that first celebrated me and Schmidt, Portugal the first to embrace us after we discovered, or rediscovered, *Saint Sebastian's Abyss,* that our first lectures, our first interviews, our first steps on the world stage were in Portugal, Lisbon in particular, Schmidt and I so young, only a few years out of the Ruskin School and the rebound from my second wife would never understand because we shared no history and she had no desire to study history because she was so deeply embedded in the now. Adding to the frustration of whether or not to publish *The Assemblage* either before or after Schmidt's *final word* on Count Hugo Beckenbauer, I was also burdened with a growing notion, that is, I began to consider the possibility of driving out or evicting, in short, *removing* the obvious rebound from my second wife from my very expensive apartment and consequently my entire life because her behavior, specifically the television and the gossip and the obsession with both my and Schmidt's acolytes, was harming my mental health, severely so, and having the obvious rebound from my second wife walking and speaking, even *breathing,* inside my prohibitively expensive apartment in a city too expensive for most was tormenting me on a constant basis and I dreamt of solitude, in fact repeated the word *solitude* to myself throughout the day like a mantra, *solitude,* I'd whisper, *solitude,* I'd repeat, *solitude,* I'd say, attempting to coax some form of seclusion into being simply by invoking the word itself. *Solitude,* I'd softly mumble, *without you I'll die.*

70

Arriving in Berlin after a pilgrimage to Upper Bavaria where he'd gone to venerate the Black Madonna in Altötting, Klaus Vogel, a young Jesuit priest, paid for a night's lodging in a boarding house on the outskirts of the city while arrangements at the cathedral where he would serve were being prepared and all of these details, trite, trivial, and everyday details, occasioned Vogel's meeting with the dying Beckenbauer, who, separated by a thin wall, was succumbing to late-stage syphilis, although it was now closer to *final-stage* or *last-stage* syphilis since he'd had late-stage syphilis for years and the disease had progressed considerably from what he'd first endured during his stays in Düsseldorf, so this *final-* or *last-stage* syphilis was horrific, Beckenbauer visited by rampant fevers, paralysis, and boils, not to mention the hallucinations that plagued the artist in an almost ceaseless barrage, the hallucinations the only available gateway to sight since Beckenbauer had been blind for over a year and these hallucinations had Beckenbauer crying out to angels and phantoms, all sorts of outlandish appeals, pleading for death or anything approximating death, any respite from the unremitting horror and on the other side of the wall lay Klaus Vogel, sensitive, God-fearing, wholly demonstrative in his beliefs, who had, in fact, recently taken a vow of chastity and poverty; he lay down to sleep only to arise upon hearing the suffering coming through the thin wall, what he later described as a *jagged moaning*, and contained inside that *jagged moaning*, at least in Vogel's mind, was *an ardent plea for salvation.* In the hall stood the innkeeper, a nasty sort, as potbellied as he was ill-tempered, who began kicking Beckenbauer's door, which, in essence, was *his* door, but it was late at night and he was drunk and hence kicking the door, whomever's door it may have been, made perfect sense. Vogel appeased the innkeeper, promising to assist the suffering man, and once he'd groused and griped he, meaning the innkeeper, disappeared upstairs and Vogel admitted himself into Beckenbauer's room. Decades later, after a long career serving God in Europe and on several missions to India, Vogel recalled this incident in his journals, published posthumously as *Vindication: In God's Arms,* journals he spent the last decade of his life composing in the foothills of Himachal Pradesh where he'd taken a vow of silence. This is how Count Hugo Beckenbauer's scene of death was revealed, passed down, and made known to us, meaning Schmidt, me, and the rest of the world.

71

At the Brandenstach all appeared calm. Seeing none of Schmidt's disciples from the back of the taxi, I approached; the doorman was expecting me because I'd called that morning to see if Schmidt was awake and well enough to receive visitors. Schmidt lived on the third floor, had lived on the third floor since selling his parents' home and leaving Austria almost a decade earlier. The doorman, sullen, elderly, dressed in a drab gray suit, had a pleasant German intonation to his English. I declined the elevator, choosing the stairs instead, teeth clenched, no longer able to feel my limbs, astonished the moment had arrived. *The moment has arrived, I told myself, I'm in Berlin, climbing the stairs of Schmidt's building, the Brandenstach, moments from facing Schmidt on his deathbed, each step I take, in fact, is a step higher and thus closer to Schmidt. And what will he say?* I wondered. *Will he merely reiterate what he said in his email? With death at his door will he finally want to reconcile? Will I find an angry Schmidt or a forgiving Schmidt or perhaps a bombastic settling-of-accounts Schmidt?* At the threshold of the door I paused, tried to discern any sounds from the other side: breathing, a conversation, his familiar cough, anything, but I heard only the dull drone of an air conditioner or a medical device.

72

Was it Klaus Vogel's charitable disposition and natural piety that urged him to save Beckenbauer's soul? What could be better, the aspiring Vogel likely thought, than a glorious and beatific deathbed conversion? Or was it an act of self-indulgence, the young priest forcing his inflexible beliefs upon a dying man? *Vindication: In God's Arms*, the posthumous collection of Vogel's journals, gives the impression that Vogel was quite eager to administer a conversion whether Beckenbauer was willing or not, to press the dying artist to embrace the divine and accept God into his life, to, in Vogel's mind, save a soul from the fires of hell at the last moment, allowing it to take flight like a glorious dove toward paradise. Vogel writes: *Upon closing the door I discerned the walls of the room, which quivered in the yellow candlelight. On a straw mattress I saw the shape of the dying man lying on his side. Small gasps escaped from his lips, as if he were astonished at where he found himself. Son of God, I spoke, stepping closer, you are not alone. The man thrashed his arms, suddenly sat up, and screamed. I saw that he was blind, a rag tied over his eyes. Boils covered the majority of his skin and I considered fetching the closest doctor but felt certain the man wouldn't make it through the night. It was at this moment that my rectitude and perseverance would be tested. A man of God stays, I told myself, a man of God offers solace and succor for all God's creatures. How could I accept the path I had chosen if I failed this test? And I recalled the Gospel of Luke and the penitent thief. I remembered my elders, who had assisted so many amidst* the Black Death, and instantly I felt the chill of divinity penetrate my flesh and enter my soul. For the first time I felt God calling me directly, and I was compelled to stay. I found a stool and sat beside the mattress where the man had collapsed, unconscious. Around the room were perhaps a dozen unfinished paintings, the blind man's works, I assumed, works of madness and delirium. A still life of a flagon; another of a vase filled with dead flowers; a nature scene that displayed, it appeared, the Carpathian foothills where a circle of plump and naked women danced. A crooked painting of a strange animal, part wolf, part bull, baring sharpened teeth, its elongated horns pointing toward a wall of flames. These were the works of a man crying out for redemption, I told myself, a man whose soul was adrift in the eternal gulf, the gulf that separated good from evil, the atoned and the condemned, the fiery gulf one must cross to be saved. And I knew my stay at the inn was my destiny just as I knew God had called to me moments before, and I had heard and accepted this call, devoting myself to saving this man's eternal soul and helping him cross the infernal crevasse. Vogel spent the next five hours giving comfort to Beckenbauer, who had no desire for comfort and, likewise, no desire to hear Vogel's biblical sermons or Vogel's exhortations about God's grace and the blessings of conversion, no time to hear Vogel's obstinate insistence that he turn toward the *lucent face of the Almighty,* that he go from *unbelieving* to *believing;* each time Vogel began to recite a gospel Beckenbauer would swing in the direction of the voice, nearly always missing, connecting only once, in fact, and sending both men tumbling to the floor. In general though, Beckenbauer lay unconscious and despite the dying man's disease and its attendant repellence, Vogel was scrupulously attentive to his needs.

73

I knocked on Schmidt's door and was instantly met by Schmidt's familiar voice urging whoever it was to come in. Don't stand on ceremony! he yelled. This was followed quickly by his all-too-familiar cough. Opening the door, I found myself in the pale dark, a room of solemn emptiness illuminated only by candles. In the center of the room stood a large bed with an immense, droning machine beside it and in the center of the bed lay Schmidt, pale and bony, all angles. The flickering of the candles across his skin was terrifying. The sockets of his sunken eyes were hollowed out, making it difficult to find the pupils in the center and when I finally found them, they were studying me. You've gained weight, he said, clicking his tongue. He began to cough and wheeze and I stood in silence watching. You received my email, he finally said, collecting himself, I was hoping to last until you got here, but, as you see, he said, I'm dying. Yes, that's been decided. I'm a hopeless case. I wanted to settle things before I passed. That email, well, forgive me for my rage, but the anger has not subsided from that bullshit you spewed in New York City, what's it been, a decade? A decade and a half? And your books, he said, especially your latter books, absurd books about *Saint Sebastian's Abyss*, crimes of art criticism, I'm sorry, but that's what they are, *crimes of art criticism,* and when a person commits crimes they must be held accountable, they must be taken to task and who will do it besides me? Who knows the inner workings of your soul better than I? And Schmidt would've continued, I'm sure, but his lungs refused and he bent sideways as a nurse appeared from the back of the apartment, entering through a pair of plastic tarps hung like curtains, crossing the enormous room in militant strides to slap Schmidt's back and assist Schmidt in expelling the phlegm that had collected and with each reprieve Schmidt's gaunt face, red from exertion, berated me. Our *disciples*, he lamented (*more coughs, more phlegm*), both yours and mine, nitwits, halfwits, dimwits (*more coughs, more phlegm*), ridiculous, I know that, but yours infinitely more ridiculous than mine because they believe in you and your books more than me and my books, but you want everything, you always have (*more coughs, more phlegm*), you want everyone to be your friend, you want to criticize art but not *offend*, which is *ludicrous*, you want to exalt yourself, the art critic, while telling everyone else their opinions are just as valid, when their opinions, you and I both know, are *less* valid, in fact their opinions are *valueless*. The critic is the one who bestows value upon the work and that's not (*more coughs, more phlegm*) a shared act. You can't stand the thought of making enemies but if you don't make enemies you aren't a critic because the sign of a good critic is the number of enemies they have and the quality of those enemies, and do you think, he managed, gasping for air, chest rattling, do you honestly believe Count Hugo Beckenbauer was afraid of making enemies? And here the nurse interceded, insisted I wait in the kitchen, through the plastic tarps, she instructed, down the hall on the right, as more phlegm, she explained, had to be expelled, which was the purpose of the large, droning machine with countless tubes attached to it. I sat at the kitchen table, everything sterile, everything also covered in plastic, listened as the nurse slapped Schmidt's back, more wheezing, more coughs, more *struggles* to cough, struggles to dislodge whatever was caught in his chest, coughs like a thousand battalions and me in the gloomy kitchen, everything packed away in boxes, the counters covered in plastic as if, in Schmidt's mind, death had already arrived, had settled down and made itself at home, or perhaps Schmidt saw death merely as a sabbatical from which he would shortly return. Presently the coughing subsided and the nurse came back, explaining in dictatorial German that Schmidt could talk for only a few more minutes as it was becoming more difficult for him to breathe and I returned hoping Schmidt was through with the dressing down and wanted, as I wanted, a reconciliation. And I stood stock-still before a dissipated Schmidt; never before had I been in such proximity to death; I saw it crouched in the corner, eyes narrowed, tapping its nails; the air had altered too, become stagnant, almost absent altogether, as if the oxygen had been suctioned out by death's soft assault and death makes itself known, I realized, by the silent and visceral struggle for life, by the *absence* of life and anyone present in that room would have known just as I knew Schmidt's time was swiftly waning.

74

There was a five-hour struggle, a five-hour *tussle* between Klaus Vogel and Count Hugo Beckenbauer, Vogel attempting to convert Beckenbauer to belief and Beckenbauer retreating into unbelief or disbelief because all Beckenbauer cared about, Vogel writes, was having sex. *Death was watching us from the doorway*, Vogel writes, *and amid his suffering all this helpless sinner, this deranged lunatic, cared about was copulation and I knew the devil had taken his soul and my opportunity was withering before my eyes.* This night, a seemingly never-ending night, a night of war waged between belief and nonbelief, God and the devil, benevolence and rancor, if anything confirmed to Vogel his life's calling even though the litany of *Our Fathers* and *Hail Marys* and *valleys of the shadow of death* ostensibly meant nothing to Beckenbauer, who, having lost all the movement in his limbs, lay supine on the fetid straw mattress, a fervent erection rising from the sheets like a tenacious flag and the only sign, in fact, that he hadn't given up. And Vogel, barely twenty years old, presiding over this stranger, reciting prayers and Psalms, chanting verses and quoting saints, eventually pressed his palms upon Beckenbauer's blazing temples and pleaded for God to release this man's soul, to forgive him his many trespasses. And slowly, ponderously, the night passed. The sounds of the early morning lodgers emerged, the shuffling of feet, the banging of water bowls, and the clearing of throats, all the daily ablutions began to resound, returning the young man to the physical world. Vogel writes: *Finally, just past dawn, the madman, who I later discovered was named Hugo Beckenbauer, died. I can't be certain on what shore of the great river his soul finally disembarked. I was still an apprentice and hadn't seen enough of life or death to know for sure. Before I called for the doctor I rekindled the fire on the stove, took those atrocious paintings, and burned them. The man was buried, I heard, the next day, although I had already departed to begin my work at the cathedral in Nikolaiviertel.*

75

Poor doomed Schmidt. Even his mustache, the feature he brandished most when angry or passionate, looked anemic. New York City, he said, remember what you said and later wrote? I nodded. And do you regret what you said? I nodded. And wrote? I nodded again. Say it, he said. Of course I regret what I said, I said, and to myself I thought, I don't *not* mean it, but I also don't really mean it either. Because I didn't really care one way or the other. Regretting something and *saying* you regretted something were immaterial to me; I simply wanted Schmidt and I to be reunited, to once again be friends and to talk passionately about the apocalypse and Dutch Mannerism and the glory of *Saint Sebastian's Abyss* like we had at Oxford, at the Ruskin School, and if it was as simple as taking something I'd both said and written back then so be it. Schmidt seemed appeased. He began to talk about his *final word* on *Saint Sebastian's Abyss* and Count Hugo Beckenbauer, and the research he'd done, mostly in Bilbao, on the Iberian Peninsula, the things he'd discovered that would indeed be the *final word* since they would put so many of the sordid rumors to rest, the things he had decided not to publish but to *bequeath* to me instead as a gift for our years of friendship, the early and middle years, of course, not the later years, which were a real travesty, the years when I'd married those *absolute bitches*, he gasped, one a lowbrow, the other a pseudoscholar immersed in the *forensics of garbage*, but he'd decided, he said, that if I flew to see him in Berlin and regretted what I'd both said and written then he would *bequeath* me what he'd discovered, and he now saw fit to do just that. And what, I asked, are you bequeathing? Schmidt fell into another spasm of coughs and once again the nurse thrust her head from behind the plastic tarp, glaring at each of us with mute severity, but Schmidt, feeling her presence, waved her away and part of me believed the enormous machine had done its work, for Schmidt seemed slightly reinvigorated. WFG, Schmidt panted, WFG, he repeated, the *initials*? The bottom of *Saint Sebastian's Abyss*, he asked, beneath the black cliff face? And my heart fell and I could see Schmidt's glee at my heart falling, which, to him, probably looked more like an enormous, all-consuming shudder than anything else because I knew exactly what he meant and that he'd found the meaning of the dedication or, more precisely, who the dedication was for. The Iberian Peninsula? I asked. A long story, he said, his lips speckled with blood, his thin mustache caked with it. I'd die simply telling you, but I'll just say that once I'd discovered the root of the initials, once I had categorical proof of the initials WFG and their meaning, or namesake, each book you wrote made you look more foolish, more ignorant of the only subject you ever cared about and I was no longer angry, no, I didn't feel anger, I felt pity, pity for you and your terrible books written not only badly but in the *wrong direction,* books written not *toward* but *away* from *Saint Sebastian's Abyss.* More coughing. More phlegm. The nurse approaching. A dispute about the machine and attaching the tube, the apparatus intended to assist his breathing. Schmidt refusing. Schmidt insisting the nurse leave him be, a defiant gleam in his eyes. The nurse withdrawing into the shadows. I discovered it all, he eventually managed, Schmidt unable to sit upright, on his side instead with the metal pan clasped to his chest, the metal pan covered in blood and phlegm. I discovered the meaning of the initials and it changed everything, the holy donkey, the serpent, the burning city, which, incidentally, is neither burning nor a city. No, we got it all wrong and the initials confirmed that. And the two lesser works, he said, aren't lesser but *more*, more important, more transcendent, once you understand the three letters and understand, of course, the context of the three letters. You'll finally understand the light of God and the meaning of Christ. *Christ?* I said. We were wrong about everything, he spat, his lips crimson and glistening. *Everything!* he roared. *Everything!* he shrieked, a string of blood hanging from his chin, his face deformed, his eyes aghast. But a critic without principles wouldn't even know he had gotten it wrong, he said, let alone *backward*. Oh yes, the light of God and the grandeur of belief and when your soul sees the light, a fervent light, a light without equal, the majestic light of God that is never-ending and resplendent, a light that ignites the spirit in luminous glory, then you'll know, and Schmidt, gasping like a diver who'd surfaced after too long, looked both triumphant and ill, more alive and more feeble than I'd ever seen, both at once. And I let you write your books and enjoy your acolytes, he gasped, who were a little more foolish than *my* acolytes because they chose you over me. And the initials? I asked. I have it all, he said, all the research immaculately accumulated in my mind, and he attempted to laugh, which swelled into coughs, which led to another argument with the nurse, this one in German, about the machine and the tubes and having me leave and Schmidt, in a valiant effort against death, sat up and waved her away, his eyes like voids, more deranged and hopeless than I'd thought possible, but determined too, gleaming like bayonets, shivering like fevers and of course this was what death looked like, I told myself, behold death! Death was a ghost in disguise, a tedious chore relegated unsparingly to each of us. Schmidt winced. I was going to write about it in my final book, he panted, my *final word* on Count Hugo Beckenbauer and *Saint Sebastian's Abyss* but I couldn't, I hadn't the fortitude, I hadn't the mettle of my youth, so I planned to tell you, he said, if you came and asked for forgiveness, which you have and I'll give you the one thing you need, which is the location and the address that will explain the initials and if you'll just be patient I'll get it out. He gasped. He vomited blood. And then Schmidt on his back, gazing at the ceiling and the nurse shuffling me into the kitchen, insisting in highly militarized German I *stay put.* And I expected to hear more coughs, more struggles, arguments at least, or the droning of that enormous machine parked like a car inside his living room but there was nothing left to struggle *for* since Schmidt had died.

76

Schmidt left behind no instructions, no information on his research, no details regarding the evidence or the reasoning behind the initials. The address and location, wherever and whatever they were related to, were never divulged, never written down. He'd had his papers burned the previous month and in his will he left everything, including various properties, not to a college or museum or to the study of Count Hugo Beckenbauer's three existing works but to an obscure church outside Vienna. And none of this, meaning the *address* and *location*, was I able to ascertain because Schmidt's lungs and throat had filled with blood and it seemed the most perverse joke, to be so close and never find out, and his drivel about the light of God and Christ even more perverse. It was nonsense, I told myself, it had to be nonsense. And I asked myself: should I write more books about *Saint Sebastian's Abyss* if the books are, as Schmidt claimed, not approaching *Saint Sebastian's Abyss* but taking me further away from *Saint Sebastian's Abyss*, books that are, in fact, insults to *Saint Sebastian's Abyss*? Schmidt had put a bug in my ear, he'd poisoned my soul; how could I write anything knowing what I, ostensibly, didn't know? The knowledge of my own ignorance made me culpable. And I traversed the Iberian Peninsula and looked for whatever it was Schmidt had discovered. I scoured Bilbao and Toledo and Málaga, the museums as well as the administrative offices and official archives in each of those cities and came out with not only nothing but less than nothing since I was more confused than when I'd begun. Had Beckenbauer once lived there? Had a collector taken the three works there after the great fire? What the fuck was on the Iberian Peninsula? Beckenbauer's name was nowhere to be found. I traveled to the villages in Catalonia, to the larger cities. I spent a week in Tarragona. A month in Zaragoza. I scoured the Basque Country. I did this for three long years until one day I discovered I wasn't very interested anymore, something inside me had broken or perhaps I'd died along with Schmidt and simply hadn't noticed, I couldn't tell, but I no longer felt anything for Count Hugo Beckenbauer or *Saint Sebastian's Abyss* or the two lesser works, also known as the *monkey paintings*, which Schmidt had insisted were not actually lesser but *more*, more important and superior. I didn't care. A sort of spiritual deadening had overcome me, a shroud of apathy so vast I didn't have the energy to find its source. For three years I tramped through Spain and Portugal, utterly anesthetized, numb to my own half-hearted research, which was perfunctory at best, indifferent to art, art criticism, even the acolytes, mine and Schmidt's, who had seamlessly moved on with their lives, Schmidt dead two years, three years, his celebrated name, *both* our celebrated names buried in the soft sands of disregard. Must I reconcile myself to the fact that my entire existence is now in question, I asked, must I consider the idea that all of it was meaningless or, worse even, replete with a meaning that was misconstrued and never understood? How could the *light of God* and *Christ* have anything to do with *Saint Sebastian's Abyss* when we'd dedicated our lives to proving that they didn't? I visited Barcelona, the Museu Nacional d'Art de Catalunya to be specific, the Rudolf Gallery to be more specific than that, but I felt nothing, felt drawn instead to my expensive apartment in my expensive city, felt it calling me home. The thought of my empty apartment with its walls of books, the luxurious loneliness that awaited, kept persisting. A weariness had taken hold of me, rather spectacularly I should add, with bouts of brooding and nightlong walks and a certain mythic shade to my features that they'd never before possessed, but all the same it was weariness and as spectacular as it may have looked, I was alone in the world. And I cursed the very solitude I longed for because I didn't want to be alone yet couldn't stand anything *but* being alone. I hated it and needed it, both at once, or at intervals, I'm not sure which, both the solitude and the discomfort I felt in my solitude, but, in any event, life became unfathomable and was this, I wondered, the suffering one experiences before achieving clarity and wisdom? Was madness the precursor to enlightenment? Out of loyalty, believing I should stay, I rented a room in Barcelona, but the room felt sluggish and claustrophobic and in an attempt to dislodge whatever was stuck inside me I visited Beckenbauer's works one last time. And in Barcelona, in the Rudolf Gallery, standing before *Saint Sebastian's Abyss*, I felt neither glory nor joy nor the sense that my limbs were being lopped off and certainly no *flood of emotions*. I stared into the eyes of the holy donkey but found neither hope nor passion, mercy nor grace, none of the emotions that had marked my soul, not even the flames in Schmidt's eyes that had blazed like dying suns; I saw instead a vacant abyss, a field of famine, and knew I would fly home and never come back because staring at *Saint Sebastian's Abyss* I saw the unadorned truth, a truth so pure it had blinded Beckenbauer and in that space, in the Rudolf Gallery, all the annihilation in the universe stood glimmering before me in the perilous promise of a dead canvas.

BIBLIOGRAPHIES

Narrator:

Heaven's Purge
Hem of the Apostles
Byzantine Dawn
Serpent's Pastoral
Harlequin's Affection
Hugo's Paradox
Weeping Sable: An Essay
Still Life with Lucifer
Left of Splendor
The Assemblage
(Unpublished) *Shroud of the Donkey*

Schmidt:

August in Rhapsody
The Gospels of Count Hugo
The Descent
The Farmhouse
Turbulent Incoherence
Bread and Death
Pale Darkness (collected essays on art,
Düsseldorf, and the Black Plague)
Sullied Kingdom
Almagest

For Further Reading:

Vindication: In God's Arms by Klaus Vogel

The Sins of Hugo's Saints by Tristan Molyneaux

Razed Effigy by Tristan Molyneaux

Grief and Doubt by Adolfas Makarov

The Diaries of Helga Heidel (edited by Franz Holfenbach,
with an afterword by Elain Baswitz)

ACKNOWLEDGMENTS

For love and support,

Richard and Janice Haber

Judy Haber

Erra Davis (The Pea)

The amazing folks at Coffee House Press who make it happen: Anitra Budd, Lizzie Davis, Daley Farr, Kellie Hultgren, Rob Keefe, Zoë Koenig, Enrique Olivarez, Courtney Rust, Erika Stevens, Marit Swanson, Carla Valadez, and Quynh Van, as well as Nina Perrota, Annemarie Eayrs, and Laurie Herrmann

Kyle Hunter for the design

Danielle Bukowski, my agent

For stalwart friendship,

Marco Antonio Alcala, Chloe Aridjis, Andrea Bajani, Matt Bell, Jennifer Blanco, Philip Boehm, Laura Calaway, Chris Cander, Edward Carey, Caroline Casey, Ryan Chapman, Budha Chowdhury, Heather Cleary, Taylor Davis-Van Atta, Danielle Diamond, Hernan Diaz, Thu Doan, Rikki Ducornet, John Earle, Will Evans, Chad Felix, Elizabeth Figueroa, Chris Fischbach, Fernando Flores, Carlos Fonesca, Tobey Forney, Rodrigo Fresán, Laura Graveline (ThunderDome), Gabe Habash, Cameron Dezon Hammon, Rodrigo Hasbún, Matt Henneman, Natalia Heredia, Michael Holtman, Sophie Hughes, Laird Hunt, Guillermo Jiménez, Kim Kiefer, Tynan Kogane, Dustin Kurtz, Hilary Leichter, Valerie Miles, Robin Myers, David Naiman, Adam Newton, Efrén Ordoñez, Keaton Patterson, Daniel and Sophia Peña (thanks for the tips in German), Jamie Portwood, Chad Post, Joy Preble, Robert Rea, João Reis, Ron Restrepo, Martin Riker, Spencer Ruchti, Adam Ehrlich

Sachs, Barbara and Pablo Ruiz, Patrick Saunders, Kit Schluter, Amy Shaughnessy, Stephen Sparks, Traci Lavois Thiebaud, Cristina Tortarolo, David Ulin, Allan Vorda

Special gratitude to the Zybècksz Archives at the Horner Institute for the time, space, and resources necessary to research my work (funded by a generous endowment from the Auchenbach Fund).

FUNDER ACKNOWLEDGMENTS

Coffee House Press is an internationally renowned independent book publisher and arts nonprofit based in Minneapolis, MN; through its literary publications and *Books in Action* program, Coffee House acts as a catalyst and connector—between authors and readers, ideas and resources, creativity and community, inspiration and action.

Coffee House Press books are made possible through the generous support of grants and donations from corporations, state and federal grant programs, family foundations, and the many individuals who believe in the transformational power of literature. This activity is made possible by the voters of Minnesota through a Minnesota State Arts Board Operating Support grant, thanks to the legislative appropriation from the Arts and Cultural Heritage Fund. Coffee House also receives major operating support from the Amazon Literary Partnership, Jerome Foundation, McKnight Foundation, Target Foundation, and the National Endowment for the Arts (NEA). To find out more about how NEA grants impact individuals and communities, visit www.arts.gov.

Coffee House Press receives additional support from Bookmobile; Dorsey & Whitney LLP; Elmer L. & Eleanor J. Andersen Foundation; Fredrikson & Byron, P.A.; the Matching Grant Program Fund of the Minneapolis Foundation; Mr. Pancks' Fund in memory of Graham Kimpton; the Schwab Charitable Fund; and the U.S. Bank Foundation.

THE PUBLISHER'S CIRCLE OF
COFFEE HOUSE PRESS

Publisher's Circle members make significant contributions to Coffee House Press's annual giving campaign. Understanding that a strong financial base is necessary for the press to meet the challenges and opportunities that arise each year, this group plays a crucial part in the success of Coffee House's mission.

Recent Publisher's Circle members include many anonymous donors, Patricia A. Beithon, Anitra Budd, Andrew Brantingham, Dave & Kelli Cloutier, Mary Ebert & Paul Stembler, Jocelyn Hale & Glenn Miller, the Rehael Fund-Roger Hale/Nor Hall of the Minneapolis Foundation, Randy Hartten & Ron Lotz, Dylan Hicks & Nina Hale, William Hardacker, Kenneth & Susan Kahn, Stephen & Isabel Keating, the Kenneth Koch Literary Estate, Cinda Kornblum, Jennifer Kwon Dobbs & Stefan Liess, the Lambert Family Foundation, the Lenfestey Family Foundation, Sarah Lutman & Rob Rudolph, the Carol & Aaron Mack Charitable Fund of the Minneapolis Foundation, Gillian McCain, Malcolm S. McDermid & Katie Windle, Mary & Malcolm McDermid, Daniel N. Smith III & Maureen Millea Smith, Peter Nelson & Jennifer Swenson, Enrique & Jennifer Olivarez, Alan Polsky, Robin Preble, Jeffrey Sugerman & Sarah Schultz, Nan G. Swid, Grant Wood, and Margaret Wurtele.

For more information about the Publisher's Circle and other ways to support Coffee House Press books, authors, and activities, please visit www.coffeehousepress.org/pages/donate or contact us at info@coffeehousepress.org.

MARK HABER is the author of the 2008 story collection *Deathbed Conversions* and the novel *Reinhardt's Garden*, long-listed for the 2020 PEN/Hemingway Award. He is the operations manager at Brazos Bookstore in Houston, Texas. His nonfiction has appeared in the *Rumpus, Music & Literature*, and *LitHub*. His fiction has appeared in *Southwest Review* and *Air/Light*.

Saint Sebastian's Abyss was designed by
Bookmobile Design & Digital Publisher Services.
Text is set in Vendetta OT.